"Lila, I want to know the truth," Jessica said in a horrified whisper. "What are we doing in Kiddie Paradise?

"Babysitting," Lila mumbled.

"Babysitting?"

"Well, not exactly babysitting," Lila amended. "We're camp counselors."

"Camp counselors in Kiddie Paradise?" Jessica screamed. "Why? How? Why didn't you tell me?"

"Two counselors dropped out at the last minute. My parents volunteered me and a friend."

"A friend?" Jessica asked. "I wouldn't do this to my worst enemy! This was supposed to be the best vacation of my life. I'm in the Caribbean. My clothes are in Miami. And I have to spend the week in Munchkin Land, taking care of little monsters?"

"Look at it from my point of view, Jess. How would you like to be stuck here watching kids all week, all by yourself? This wasn't my idea! I'm here against my will, too."

Jessica shook her head. "Oh, no. It's not the same thing at all. You lied to me! You got me here under false pretenses!"

"I'm sorry, Jess," Lila said with a sniffle. "But you're my very closest friend, and I thought you would understand. We may be stuck here with a bunch of screaming brats, but at least we've got each other."

"Oh, no!" Jessica said. "I may be stuck with you, but I'll never forgive you for this. I'm never speaking to you again!"

SWEET VALLEY
High.

THE BOYFRIEND
WAR

Written by
Kate William

Created by
FRANCINE PASCAL

BANTAM BOOKS
NEW YORK · TORONTO · LONDON · SYDNEY · AUCKLAND

RL 6, age 12 and up

THE BOYFRIEND WAR
A Bantam Book / March 1996

Sweet Valley High® is a registered trademark of Francine Pascal
Conceived by Francine Pascal
Produced by Daniel Weiss Associates, Inc.
33 West 17th Street
New York, NY 10011
Cover art by Bruce Emmett

ISBN: 0-553-57035-8

Published simultaneously in the United States and Canada

Bantam Books are published by Bantam Books, a division of Bantam
Doubleday Dell Publishing Group, Inc. Its trademark, consisting of the
words "Bantam Books" and the portrayal of a rooster, is Registered in
U.S. Patent and Trademark Office and in other countries. Marca
Registrada. Bantam Books, 1540 Broadway, New York, New York 10036.

PRINTED IN THE UNITED STATES OF AMERICA

OPM   0 9 8 7 6 5 4 3 2 1

To Michelle Gurevich

Chapter 1

"Mind if I join you?" asked Caroline Pearce, setting her lunch tray on the cafeteria table. Her red curls bounced as she sat next to Jessica Wakefield without waiting for a reply.

"Sure, Caroline," Amy Sutton replied, fanning her face with her napkin. She pointed to the roasted chicken on Caroline's tray. "How can you eat *hot* lunch today? It's ninety degrees out!"

Jessica glanced at Lila Fowler and rolled her eyes. She wasn't in the mood for Caroline's gossip today—she was too busy thinking about her own wonderful life to listen to stories about other people. But it was Friday, the last day before spring break. And Jessica was really too excited to care who was sitting next to her.

"Did you hear about our vacation plans?" Jessica asked Caroline, figuring she might as well give the class gossip the juiciest news in town.

"Of course," Caroline said smugly. She turned to

1

Lila. "Your uncle Jimmo owns a Club Paradise in the Caribbean, and he had two cancellations for next week, so you asked Jessica to come along. Am I missing anything?"

"Only the best spring break anyone ever had!" Jessica boasted. "Lila and I will be lying on the shores of the Caribbean for a whole week, showing off our new bathing suits. At least, *I'll* be showing off *my* new bathing suit. Lila, you really should have come shopping with me and Amy last night."

"I told you, I didn't need a new bathing suit. I just bought a pink bikini on Monday," Lila said.

"But you didn't get to see the fabulous red dress I found at Bibi's, for dancing all night with the gorgeous guys at Club Paradise!"

"Sorry," Lila said, "but my mother wanted me to go out to dinner with her."

"You're forgiven," Jessica said magnanimously. "In fact," she added, with a look around the table, "any friend who offers to take me to Club Paradise is forgiven for everything—forever."

"I'll keep that in mind," Lila said dryly.

Jessica grinned. "It's too bad the rest of you have to spend the week sweating through the worst heat wave ever to hit Sweet Valley—it's supposed to get hotter and hotter all week long. Meanwhile, Lila and I will be living it up in Jamaica with tons of great-looking boys!"

"Thanks a lot, Jess," Amy said. She turned to Caroline. "Excessive bragging is a defense mechanism," she explained.

"Oh, no!" Jessica cried gleefully. "It's more of

2

Amy's Project Youth psychobabble!"

Amy ignored her. "And making fun of people," she continued, "is a way to mask the guilt a person feels when *she* gets an amazing opportunity and her friends are left out in the cold."

"Or in this case, the *heat*," Lila said, though she seemed as cool and comfortable as she always did.

Jessica flashed Amy a look of mock concern. "I'm sorry, Amy. Aren't I being empathic and sensitive?"

"About as empathic and sensitive as the person who scheduled spring break during a week when it'll be too hot even to lie on the beach," Amy complained. "What am I going to do all week? After our spending spree last night, Jess, I'm too broke to go to the mall—not that it would be much fun without you two. To top it off, Barry's going to Palm Springs."

"Gee, that's rough," Caroline said, obviously fishing for gossip. "Are you two having problems? I can't believe your boyfriend would desert you like that."

"It's nothing like that," Amy assured her quickly. "He's going on vacation with his family. And with Jessica and Lila going away, too, there won't be anything to do around here!"

"That's for sure," Jessica agreed cheerfully. She took a bite of her apple and chewed it thoughtfully before continuing. "The only person who seems happy about being stuck in Sweet Valley for the week is Elizabeth. She's excited about some honors project for English class."

Amy shook her head. "I don't know how you ended up with a twin sister who thinks doing school-work is a fun way to spend a vacation! And it's not even *required* schoolwork. Why does a brain like Liz need extra credit?"

"You know my sister. She never settles for a plain old A when she can get an A-plus!"

"If you and Elizabeth weren't mirror images," Caroline said, looking across the cafeteria at Jessica's twin, "nobody would believe you're from the same planet, let alone the same family!"

Jessica followed Caroline's gaze to a table near the windows. She tried to consider her sister with an objective eye. "Mirror images" was an apt description. *Of course, Elizabeth isn't quite as gorgeous as I am,* she told herself. *But that's only because she doesn't make the most of her natural beauty, like I do.* Jessica was always urging Elizabeth to wear her shoulder-length, golden-blond hair loose and sexy. But sensible Elizabeth insisted on pulling it back from her face in a more casual look. Even in today's heat, Jessica wouldn't be seen in public in a boring ponytail—this morning, she had spent nearly an hour twisting her hair into a cool but glamorous French braid.

Elizabeth's loose cotton blouse was a pretty shade of yellow, Jessica admitted. But steamy weather was a marvelous excuse to wear something really sexy, like Jessica's hot-pink halter. For some reason, looking sexy was never high on Elizabeth's list of priorities. Just as schoolwork was never high on Jessica's list.

Caroline's voice broke in on her reverie. "You don't look too excited, Lila." Jessica knew Caroline was looking for gossip.

But Caroline was right this time, Jessica realized. Lila didn't seem the least bit excited about the trip.

In fact, she had hardly said a word about Club Paradise since she had called Jessica on Wednesday night to invite her.

Well, Lila doesn't need this vacation half as much as I do, Jessica thought. *Lila's boyfriend wasn't killed in an accident, like poor Sam. And Lila didn't have to go through another boy's death and a crazy murderer stalking her sister.* Jessica shuddered, thinking of the horrible events of the past few months. First her boyfriend Sam Woodruff had been killed in a drunk-driving accident—and Elizabeth had been the driver. Only Jessica knew that Elizabeth had gotten drunk because Jessica spiked her punch. Before Jessica could confess to her sister, though, an evil girl who looked just like the twins had come to Sweet Valley and begun following Elizabeth. The evil look-alike had intended to kill Elizabeth and take over her identity. Jessica had stopped her just in time.

Now Elizabeth and Jessica were the best of friends again. But that didn't mean they saw eye to eye on things like school and boys—carefree Jessica rarely paid attention to her schoolwork, concentrating instead on parties and boys. Elizabeth was a serious student and had a long-term boyfriend, Todd Wilkins. In spite of their differences, the twins were closer than ever since the threat to Elizabeth's life.

Jessica sighed happily as she looked around the cafeteria now. *I certainly do deserve a vacation*, she thought, *and this glamorous trip will announce to the world that I'm back and happy to be alive.* She wasn't going to let Lila's lack of enthusiasm dampen her spirits.

"Oh, Lila's been rich for so long that she's used to this kind of luxury," Jessica explained airily. She thought it was sad that her best friend was too jaded to enjoy life's pleasures.

"Speaking of rich—" said Amy, looking over Jessica's shoulder.

Bruce Patman stormed by, carrying a lunch tray.

Caroline turned in her chair. "Hi, Bruce!" she called sweetly. Jessica looked at Amy and giggled. If Caroline was trying to flirt with Bruce, she was way out of her league. Dark-haired Bruce Patman was tall, gorgeous, and wealthy. And right now, he was obviously steamed about something. Bruce stalked past their table without turning.

"What's eating him?" asked Lila. "And where's his usual parade of loyal admirers?"

"He looks kind of hot under the collar to me— and I don't think it's the weather!" Jessica said. "Maybe he and Pamela had a fight."

"I don't think so," Amy said. "They looked pretty lovey-dovey last night at the soccer game. I heard she was leaving on a trip with her family this morning— she'll be gone all week." She laughed. "Maybe God's Gift to Women is lonely, now that he's in love and can't play the field the way he used to."

Caroline smiled mysteriously. "I know what's bothering him!"

"What?" Jessica and Amy asked together. Even Lila raised her eyebrows.

Caroline stared at them thoughtfully. "All right, I'll tell you. But you have to promise not to say a word to anyone."

6

❖　　❖　　❖

Bruce stomped through the cafeteria, carrying his lunch tray in front of him. He didn't know why he'd bothered to buy lunch that day. It was too hot to eat. But Bruce wasn't hungry anyway. Not after what he had learned at breakfast that morning.

A girl greeted him from a nearby table, but Bruce didn't stop to see who it was. The last thing he wanted right now was company—unless it was Pamela Robertson. But she was on her way to the Grand Canyon with her parents for an entire week. He wished he and his parents could go away for a boring family vacation like that. Like normal families did.

Bruce pushed open the door to the school's courtyard. Usually, it was full of students around lunchtime. Today, it was deserted. As Bruce had anticipated, the blazing heat had forced everyone inside.

Bruce slid his lunch tray onto a bench and sat down. "This can't be happening," he whispered, pounding a fist against the bench. He should have seen the situation coming. And now that he knew about it, he should be able to stop it. "Why me?"

He was more important and popular than any kid in town, he reminded himself. *I own a Porsche, for Pete's sake!* He was used to being in control. But he had no idea how to control this.

Bruce grabbed the lunch tray and hurled it away. He heard it clatter against a tree trunk and imagined that it was the sound of his whole world shattering into pieces.

"The whole junior class is getting old and boring,"

7

Enid Rollins lamented to Elizabeth and Olivia Davidson across their cafeteria table. "It's the day before spring break—and everyone is staying in town—or going away with their parents. Jessica and Lila are the only ones planning anything out of the ordinary."

"And my sister won't let anyone forget it!" Elizabeth said, laughing. "I'm happy for Jessica, but lying on the beach in an artificial paradise is not my idea of a Caribbean vacation."

"Me either!" Olivia agreed. "If I were going to the Caribbean, I'd rather stay somewhere with no tourists, where I could learn about the culture of the islands and sketch the Arawak Indian ruins. Club Paradise sounds beautiful, but I'd rather be somewhere *real*."

"I agree," Enid said stoutly. She took a long sip of chocolate milk and then laughed. "And if someone offered me an all-expense-paid vacation, I'd be on an airplane the next day!"

"Are you kidding?" Olivia said, tossing her mane of curly brown hair. "The next hour!"

"I'd go almost anywhere at this point," Elizabeth said, "just to get away from the sticky weather!"

Olivia reached for one of Enid's grapes. "So, Liz," she asked, "what are you and the dashing Mr. Wilkins planning to do over spring break?"

"We're going to the Dairi Burger after school today," Elizabeth said, "but only for an hour. Then Todd has to go home and pack his gear. He and his family leave tomorrow to go camping in Yosemite. His parents will be gone for two weeks, but Todd is flying back alone next weekend, in time for school.

8

Until then, I'm on my own—with no boyfriend and no sister."

"Poor Liz—stuck with only the two of us for company!" Enid said, laughing, to Olivia. "It must be awful for you!"

"You know I didn't mean it that way," Elizabeth protested. "I can't imagine anyone else I'd rather spend my vacation with than the two of you—though I will miss Todd." Elizabeth stirred her yogurt. "But I'm also kind of glad he's going. It will give me time to work on that honors project for English class."

"Except for when we kidnap you and force you to lighten up and have some fun," Olivia warned. "Which I plan to do for at least a couple of hours every day. Did you hear about Beat-the-Heat Week at the Plaza Theatre? All week long, they're showing special matinees of old romance movies."

Elizabeth brightened. "What's playing?"

"*Casablanca* is first, at two o'clock Monday," Olivia said. "Are you two up for it?"

"Are you kidding?" Enid asked. "Sitting in an air-conditioned movie theater watching Humphrey Bogart and Ingrid Bergman? Who said Sweet Valley would be boring next week?"

"It sounds great!" Elizabeth agreed. "It's just about my favorite movie in the whole world."

"The other movies are almost as good," Olivia promised.

"Let's go to every single one," Enid suggested.

"You're on!" said Elizabeth. "After all, I can't spend every waking moment researching my English paper."

"Is this your family-biography paper for Mr. Collins's class?" Olivia asked. "Who are you writing about?"

"I didn't realize how hard it would be to pick someone," Elizabeth admitted. "I have some pretty interesting ancestors! But I've decided to stick close to home—I'm writing about my mother."

"It must be neat to have an artist for a mother," Olivia said wistfully.

"She's an interior designer, actually."

"Well, that's a lot more artistic than managing women's sportswear at Simpson's department store," Olivia said, referring to her own mother's career.

Elizabeth caught Enid's eye and smiled. To unconventional Olivia, having to sell blazers and skirts for a living would seem like a prison sentence. Elizabeth's own wardrobe was pretty conservative, but she had always admired Olivia's artistic flair. Elizabeth helped herself to one of Enid's grapes. "I've always felt like Mom and I have a lot in common," she said. "It'll be fun to find out what she was like when she was my age."

When Elizabeth and Todd arrived at the Dairi Burger that afternoon, the popular hangout was almost full. The whole school seemed to be there to celebrate the beginning of spring break. Elizabeth spotted Jessica sitting in the back corner with Amy, Caroline, and Annie Whitman. Elizabeth waved at her twin and then began scanning the room for an empty table.

"There's a booth!" she said, pointing.

"It's right next to Patman and his loudmouth pals," Todd said, "but it looks like the only empty table. I guess we'd better snag it."

After they had ordered sodas, Todd took Elizabeth's hand in his. "I'm going to miss you, Liz," he said. "Are you sure you don't want to come along to Yosemite with us? My parents said to tell you the invitation's still open."

Elizabeth smiled and shook her head. "Thanks for asking, but I need the time to work on the English project I told you about."

Todd whistled. "Writing a paper—that's one thing you'd never catch me doing unless it was absolutely necessary."

Elizabeth laughed. "Now you sound like Jessica!"

Loud, derisive laughter suddenly came from the next booth. Over Todd's shoulder, Elizabeth could see Bruce Patman shaking his head at his friends.

"Chill out, Bruce," said Barry Rork. "I don't know what the big deal is. So what if I'm going to Palm Springs with my family? I hardly ever get a chance to be with my parents and my brother."

"What are you getting so upset about, Bruce?" asked Ken Matthews, quarterback of Sweet Valley High's football team. "Lots of kids go away with their families for spring break."

Bruce scoffed. "The operative word there is *kids.*"

"In case you haven't noticed, we *are* in high school," Ken said dryly.

"It's the law of the teenage jungle," Kirk Anderson said philosophically. "Occasionally, you have to go along with what your parents want—let them think they call the shots. I have to go see my grandmother for the week, but I'm not complaining. I'll just grin and bear it, and make the old lady happy." He winked. "Besides, my grandmother loves to hand out twenty-dollar bills."

Bruce shook his head and turned back to Ken. "So, Matthews, where is your happy little family going? Disneyland?"

Elizabeth thought Ken looked angry, but he spoke calmly. "My parents and sisters and I are driving up the coast to Monterey to visit my uncle."

Bruce jumped up, his handsome face red with fury. "You guys are losers!" he yelled. "I can't believe how pathetic you are—going on vacation with Mommy and Daddy. Why don't you grow up?"

He slammed a few dollars down on the table, next to his untouched hamburger. Then he strode out the door.

Elizabeth looked at Todd and shook her head. She didn't care how rich and powerful Bruce's family was. He had no right to criticize people that way—no right at all.

"It's bad enough when he mistreats the rest of the world," Amy said as Bruce Patman stormed out of the room. "But I've never heard him lay into his so-called friends like that!"

"Bruce has always been a freak," Jessica said with a shrug. "Who wants to talk about him, when Lila and I are leaving Sunday for Club Paradise?"

Amy sighed. She didn't want to hear again about Jessica and Lila's wonderful week.

12

"Where is Lila?" Caroline asked pointedly.

"She said her father needed her help choosing a present for her mom's birthday," Amy said.

"So, have you three figured out any plans for the week?" Jessica asked, with a twinkle in her eye.

"Unfortunately, yes," Amy lamented. "This will give you more to gloat about, Jess. Your sister and her drippy friends aren't the only ones writing family biographies this week. Mr. Collins broke the news to me today—my English grade is sunk if I don't get some extra credit. I have to pick an ancestor and write a report. Isn't that the dullest thing you've ever heard?"

"Yes," Jessica agreed. "Do you know who you're going to write about?"

"I haven't a clue," Amy said. "I don't have a single relative who's ever done anything interesting."

"Your mother's sort of a celebrity," Caroline said. "Dyan Sutton, local television sportscaster."

"Yeah, but I'm still supposed to be mad at her for grounding me last week. Jess, I know *you've* got some interesting relatives. Can I borrow one of them? I'll change the names, and Mr. Collins won't know the difference. Didn't you tell me you had a circus performer in the family?"

Jessica sipped her diet soda thoughtfully. "Actually, we've had a couple," she acknowledged. "But you're probably talking about Jessamyn Johnson, my great-great-grandmother."

"Jessamyn?" Annie asked. "You've got to be kidding. And let me guess, she had a twin sister named Elizabyn. Right?"

Jessica grinned. "Actually, her twin sister was named Elisabeth, with an *s* instead of a *z*. Jessamyn was sixteen years old when she joined the circus."

"She sounds perfect!" Amy said hopefully. "Can I borrow her for my English paper?"

Jessica shrugged magnanimously. "Go ahead. She's yours. I'll even ask Liz to keep an eye out for any old papers that might help you. After that, you can just make up anything else you need to fill in the gaps."

The engine of the black Porsche throbbed to life, and Bruce leaned back in the leather seat, closing his eyes. He waited for the rush of adrenaline he always felt when the engine engaged. For the first time since he'd owned the car of his dreams, the rush didn't come.

His fist tightened around the gearshift, but Bruce kept the car idling in the parking space. "Nothing's the same anymore!"

Everything that used to give him pleasure meant nothing to him now—his car, his money, even the coy looks from the sophomore and junior girls. He knew that those things hadn't actually changed. *He* was the one who was different. Everything he'd counted on all his life—everything that made him who he was— was crumbling to pieces.

It had all happened that morning at the breakfast table. Bruce was eating his eggs like any other morning, when his mother and father had told him the news: They were separating. His mother was moving out in a couple of weeks—maybe for good.

How could they do this? Bruce asked himself. Of course, his parents had been arguing a lot lately. But Henry and Marie Patman had been together for almost twenty years. *Why now? Why me?*

Bruce gripped the gearshift even tighter and gunned the engine again. Then he roared out of the parking lot. The familiar streets of Sweet Valley shimmered in the unseasonable heat. But all Bruce could see was his father's face as it had looked at breakfast that morning.

The most powerful man in town had a look of guilt on his face and tears in his eyes.

Chapter 2

"It's ten o'clock!" Jessica sang, bounding into the kitchen Saturday morning. "Only twenty-five more hours until my nine o'clock flight tomorrow—and then I'll be on my way to Club Paradise!"

"Twenty-three hours," Elizabeth said dryly, turning back to the counter, where she was slicing fruit for brunch.

"Who cares? I'll spend today packing an awesome wardrobe, and then spend a whole week lying on the beach, flirting with good-looking guys, and having handsome waiters bring me mineral water to drink from coconut shells!"

She filled a glass of water and sipped it, eyes closed.

"It's too bad you'll be here getting sweaty the whole time, Liz," Jessica continued. "It's going to be about three hundred degrees all week. That reminds me—can I borrow your new green bathing suit?"

"Don't you already have about four of your own?"

"Five," Jessica said, "including the bikini I bought Thursday night. That's just the point. I've got six days to spend on the beach, and only five bathing suits. You wouldn't want me to show up in the same thing twice!"

Elizabeth recoiled in mock horror. "Certainly not! What would people think?"

"Besides," Jessica continued, "I don't want to commit myself to any particular tan line."

The twins' father walked into the room, mopping his forehead with a handkerchief. "Maybe brunch wasn't such a good idea in this weather," he said. "It's really too hot out to eat."

"All we're having is cold fruit and yogurt," Elizabeth said. "It'll be ready as soon as Mom gets off the phone. She's talking to somebody about a consulting job."

"She's talking about business on a Saturday morning?" Jessica exclaimed. "I can see where you got your serious personality, Liz. It's a good thing this family has me around to keep everything in perspective."

"Is that what you do around here?" Mr. Wakefield said, sitting down at the table. "Keep things in perspective?"

"Well, of course," Jessica replied. "Somebody's got to have her priorities straight. By the way, are you sure you don't want to write about *me* for your family biography, Liz? My life's a lot more dramatic than Mom's—what with expense-paid trips to the Caribbean and all."

Jessica whirled around to set a platter of fruit on the table. Elizabeth rolled her eyes at her father.

17

Jessica was going to be impossible to live with for the next twenty-three hours.

"It's too bad the college is on a different schedule," Elizabeth said to her father. "Steven doesn't have spring break this week. I guess it'll just be you, me, and Mom sweating it out here."

"Hi, everyone!" said Alice Wakefield, hurrying into the room. Elizabeth thought she looked almost as excited as Jessica. "That was Hank Patman on the phone. His company has a subsidiary opening soon in Chicago, but there are major problems with the new plant. He's asked me to come on board as a design consultant, to take over the project and set things straight."

"That's wonderful, honey!" said her husband.

"It's a great opportunity for me to build up a track record in that part of the country," Mrs. Wakefield said. "And Hank is willing to pay me a lot of money for just a few weeks of work—though they'll be awfully busy weeks."

"I didn't know you knew Mr. Patman well enough that he'd think of you for a job like that," said Elizabeth.

Her mother turned quickly to open the refrigerator. "Sweet Valley is not that big a town," she explained. "It's not exactly crawling with interior designers."

"Everyone knows you're the best," Jessica said with a shrug. "But did you hear the really big news about Mr. Patman?"

"What big news?" Mrs. Wakefield asked.

"D-I-V-O-R-C-E!" Jessica sang loudly. "I have it on very good authority that Mr. and Mrs. Patman are separating and will probably get divorced!"

"Jessica!" her father reprimanded her. "That's not a very sensitive attitude."

"So? The Patmans are not a very sensitive family."

Elizabeth sighed. She remembered when her own parents had separated. Elizabeth, Jessica, and their older brother, Steven, had gone through several terrible weeks, fearing that a divorce was imminent. Luckily, their parents had worked through their problems.

For a moment, Elizabeth tried to feel some sympathy for Bruce. Even a jerk like him had to have feelings. Then she remembered the way he had lashed out at his friends at the Dairi Burger the night before.

"It's too bad about the Patmans," she said. "But it doesn't seem to be having any effect on Bruce. He's as arrogant and unpleasant as ever."

"Try to be sensitive, girls," Mrs. Wakefield advised. "Bruce must be going through a difficult time. I'm sure his parents are too," she added thoughtfully. "Maybe this situation in Chicago is just what Hank needs—a chance to immerse himself in a pretty intense business problem."

Elizabeth realized her mother had been calling Mr. Patman "Hank." Elizabeth had trouble thinking of Henry Wilson Patman—the formal, elegant millionaire—as plain old Hank. She couldn't imagine being on such familiar terms with a man like him.

Mr. Wakefield smiled at his wife. "I suppose this job means you'll be the invisible woman around here for a couple of weeks."

"I'm afraid so," Mrs. Wakefield replied. "We'll be working long hours on this one!"

Elizabeth slumped back in her seat, suddenly feeling drained from the heat of the morning. The job sounded like a wonderful opportunity. But Elizabeth had looked forward to spending time with her mother during spring break, interviewing her for the family-biography project.

"Poor Liz," Jessica said. "It looks like you're stuck in the house all week with just Dad! But I promise I'll send you a really nice postcard from Club Paradise."

Jessica began reciting average spring temperatures in the Caribbean, but Elizabeth tuned out. Unfortunately, she realized, Jessica was probably right about spring break at home. Things would be lonely in Sweet Valley all week. *Maybe I should have gone camping with Todd's family after all,* she thought sadly.

"I need to pack that green bathing suit you promised to lend me," Jessica said, pushing open the door to her sister's room on Saturday afternoon. "Can I have it now?"

Elizabeth looked up from her reading. "I never said you could borrow it, Jess."

"Well, you didn't get a chance to actually say so, but you were going to let me use it. So just tell me where it is—"

Elizabeth arched her eyebrows. "Oh, I was going to let you use it, was I?"

"While you get it, I'll bring my big blue suitcase in here," Jessica said quickly, flashing her most engaging smile. "You don't mind, do you? I'm out of space to pack in my own room. But you have lots of empty space in here that I can use!"

Elizabeth laughed. "Honestly, Jessica. If you'd keep your own bedroom a little neater—"

Jessica made a face as she ran back into her own room. She returned a minute later, lugging an enormous suitcase.

Elizabeth helped her set it on the bed.

"What is all this stuff?" Elizabeth asked, pulling a slinky red dress from the jumble of clothes that was piled haphazardly in the suitcase. "I thought you were going to spend the week on the beach. You know—bathing suits, shorts, T-shirts . . ."

Jessica sighed. Elizabeth was so unworldly. "You don't know anything at all about a place like Club Paradise. I'll be on the beach during the day, of course. I'll need only bathing suits and cover-ups for that. But I'll need shorts for boating, and jeans in case it gets chilly in the evenings."

"What I wouldn't give for a few chilly evenings here this week," Elizabeth said.

Jessica had more exciting things to think about than the weather in Sweet Valley. "And at night," she continued dreamily, "all the good-looking guys who saw me in my bikinis on the beach will want to take me dancing. That's what the new red dress is for— and the sequined top with the black miniskirt. Remember, Liz, this is a classy place! And I've got Lila the Millionaire Clotheshorse for competition. Though I'm so grateful to Lila for choosing me to go with her that I might even consider letting her have first pick of the boys!"

"How generous of you," Elizabeth said, rooting through the pile of clothes in the suitcase. She held

21

up a scrap of gold Lycra. "What's this—a head-band?"

"No, silly, it's the top to a bikini!"

"You've got to be kidding! Do Mom and Dad know about this?"

"Why should they?"

"So they won't be too shocked when the Caribbean Vice Squad calls to tell them you've been arrested for indecent exposure."

"In the Caribbean, people are much less uptight about these things," Jessica said in her most authoritative tone.

"I hope for your sake that the bikini stays up," Elizabeth said dryly. "And what's this blue cotton skirt for? It doesn't look like your usual style, Jess."

"It's a golf skirt, silly."

"But you don't play golf."

"Sure I do!" Jessica protested. "Well, I haven't yet," she amended. "But I do if I meet a really gorgeous guy who wants to. If I didn't bring a golf skirt, what would I wear—a tennis dress?"

"Heaven forbid," Elizabeth said. "You might be a social outcast for life! Speaking of tennis dresses, you seem to have enough of them here to outfit Wimbledon."

"I only packed three!" Jessica said. "Oh, that reminds me—I need to bring four. Can I borrow the one you bought last month, Liz? It's a little high-cut at the neckline, but the skirt flounces just right to show off my legs."

Elizabeth sighed. "You might as well," she said in a resigned tone. "I'll die of heatstroke if I so much as think about running around on a tennis court here this week."

"As long as you're finding the tennis dress, you might as well pull out the green bathing suit, too."

"Why the sudden interest in my green bathing suit?" Elizabeth asked. "I didn't think it was sexy enough to live up to your standards."

"Not from the front," Jessica explained, "but it looks really great from behind!"

"You're going to change your suit every time you want to tan your back?"

Jessica sighed, exasperated. "If I go snorkeling, I'll need a suit that looks good from the back," she explained slowly, trying to sound more patient than she felt. "Don't you know *anything*?"

"Apparently not," Elizabeth said. She pulled a sheer white blouse from the suitcase. "Is this new?" she asked. "It's kind of pretty, with the big shawl collar—almost like a built-in cape."

Jessica nodded. "I bought it the other night," she said. "It's to wear with tight jeans, for horseback riding. It'll flow gracefully behind me in the breeze as I gallop into the sunset."

"Or as you fall off the horse," Elizabeth said. "You haven't been horseback riding in years."

Leave it to Liz to think of that, Jessica thought. "Can I borrow your white bag?" she asked. "Mine has jelly stains on it."

"I guess I'd better just say yes," Elizabeth said. "I don't want to hear how you managed to do that."

"I think I need another suitcase," Jessica said, staring at the pile of clothes. "I'm never going to be able to shut this one. Can I use your suitcase, too?"

"If you fold these neatly, instead of tossing everything together like a salad, all of your clothes will fit into this suitcase—and they won't wrinkle."

"Oh, no!" Jessica screamed suddenly.

"What is it?"

"I almost forgot my suntan lotion!"

Elizabeth laughed, and Jessica gave her a dirty look.

"You never told me which Club Paradise you're going to," Elizabeth said. "Aren't there several in the Caribbean?"

"Lila says it's in Jamaica—not far from Montego Bay."

Elizabeth stared at her. "Montego Bay? Isn't that the one that's advertised as the Kiddie Club Paradise? I thought it was for families."

"No way," Jessica said. "Well, I guess a few people might bring children, but I'm sure the Kiddie Club is separate from the adult part. They wouldn't allow kids to disturb the adults' fun!"

"Maybe I have it mixed up with another location," Elizabeth said. "I hate to admit it, but I envy you, Jess. I think the temperature's shot up another five degrees here, just in the last hour. And it's supposed to be even worse tomorrow!"

For the first time that weekend, Jessica truly felt sorry for her sister—stuck alone in Sweet Valley in the terrible heat, with only drips like Enid and Olivia to keep her company.

"Gee, Liz," she said. "It's too bad you can't come, too. You deserve a vacation almost as much as I do."

"Thanks," Elizabeth said, smiling. "You even sound sincere! And you're right. You do deserve a great vacation. I really hope it's everything you're expecting it to be, Jessica. I'm looking forward to hearing all about it! Until then, I'll be going to air-conditioned movies and working on my English project."

Jessica smiled warmly. She was glad she could count on Elizabeth to be truly happy for her. Of course, it was also kind of nice to see that her sister was a little envious. Jessica supposed the least she could do was show some interest in the project Elizabeth seemed so excited about.

"What did you say your English paper is on?" Jessica asked.

"I've only told you five times."

"I was distracted," Jessica said. "I had more interesting things to worry about."

"It's the family-biography project."

"Oh, yeah. Gee, I almost forgot to mention it, but Amy has to do a biography, too. I told her you might be able to help her out a little, Liz. You're so good at all that research stuff."

Jessica crossed her fingers behind her back. Elizabeth wouldn't like it if she knew Jessica was letting Amy borrow their great-great-grandmother Jessamyn. Personally, Jessica didn't see why it mattered, but Elizabeth could be picky about anything she saw as dishonesty. Jessica preferred to let Amy break the news to her—after Jessica was safely in Jamaica with Elizabeth's green bathing suit and anything else she needed to borrow.

Luckily, Elizabeth was a naturally helpful person.

"I don't know how I can help Amy," Elizabeth said with a shrug. "After all, it's *her* family. But I guess I could answer a few questions about where to look for information."

"And who did you say you're writing about, Liz?"

"I told you. I'm researching Mom's life before she married Dad and had us kids."

Jessica rolled her eyes. "Now that sounds really exciting. Forget Club Paradise—I'm staying here! Who knows what skeletons wild and crazy Mom might have in her closet?"

"Come on, Jess!" Elizabeth protested. "We don't know everything Mom's ever done. I'll bet she's had some fascinating experiences."

"Don't hold your breath, Liz," Jessica cautioned. "Mom's an open book! Your paper will be a real snooze."

Elizabeth sighed. "Unfortunately, you may be right," she admitted. "My whole week will probably be a real snooze."

Jessica watched through the airplane window Sunday morning as the Los Angeles suburbs receded below. She leaned back into the leather seat with a contented sigh. Lila had really outdone herself this time.

"I can't believe I'm actually flying first class!" she said. "After everything else you've done, Lila, I wouldn't have minded sitting in coach."

Lila shrugged. "It's not that big a deal," she said, taking a copy of *Ingenue* magazine from a smiling flight attendant. "Just enjoy yourself."

Lila certainly didn't seem to be enjoying *herself*, Jessica noticed. It must be nice to be so used to luxury that you could take a first-class flight to the Caribbean for granted.

"You know, Lila," Jessica began, "I hate to gush, but I've got to tell you that you're a fantastic friend. I mean, you could have asked Amy or somebody else to go with you. I just want to say, for the record, how much I appreciate that you asked me."

Lila fidgeted in her seat, and Jessica realized that her best friend was surprised and embarrassed.

"Don't worry, Lila. I promise I won't be sappy anymore," she said. "That's the last time I'll thank you."

Lila turned back to her magazine, but Jessica heard her say something under her breath. Jessica couldn't be sure, but it sounded like "I'm afraid you're right."

Jessica had been in Montego Bay, Jamaica, for an entire half hour, and all she had seen so far was the luggage carousel at the airport. The same bags kept parading by, again and again.

Jessica was beginning to feel sick. The green duffel, the scuffed-up brown bag—every piece of luggage had glided by at least a dozen times. Where was Jessica's powder-blue suitcase, stuffed with carefully chosen outfits?

Lila's stylish but surprisingly small bag had shown up on the conveyor belt a good ten minutes earlier. Now it was in the firm grip of Lila's uncle Jimmo—a small, energetic man who seemed to be talking Lila's ear off.

"You're lucky to have such a loyal friend to keep you company this week, Lila," Uncle Jimmo was saying. "I hope the little monsters won't be too much for you. . . ."

Jessica wondered what kind of monsters he was talking about. Jellyfish? Mosquitoes? Teenage boys? But she was too worried about her suitcase to give the question much thought.

"I'm awfully glad you could come on such short notice," he continued. "You don't know how glad I was when your parents said you didn't have any plans for the week."

When the conveyor belt screeched to a halt, Jessica sat down on the platform, miserable. "What will I do all week without all my clothes?" she wailed.

Uncle Jimmo put a hand on her shoulder. "Don't worry, Jessica," he said. "I'm sure your bag isn't really lost—it just missed the change of planes. It's probably sitting in Miami right now, waiting for the next flight that has a little extra space."

"It'll be here in a day or two, Jessica," Lila said kindly. "Until then, you can borrow some of my shorts and things."

"But, Lila," Jessica protested, "what if the airline doesn't find it? What if all my clothes are gone forever? I never even got to show you my new red dress for wearing to the disco!"

Uncle Jimmo laughed. "I wouldn't worry about that," he said. "You'll be much too tired at night for dancing! All you'll need is a swimsuit and shorts, anyway. And I'm sure we can set you up with those until your suitcase arrives."

Jessica sighed. Uncle Jimmo was probably close to

28

forty. He couldn't possibly understand what it was like to be young. A day of sunbathing, snorkeling, and windsurfing would leave her with plenty of energy for dancing all night.

At least Lila seemed surprisingly sympathetic. More than anyone, Lila knew the importance of being dressed stylishly. Maybe she would lend Jessica a party dress.

At seven thirty on Sunday evening, the temperature in Sweet Valley was still ninety degrees. But in the Patman family dining room, Bruce felt a definite chill—whenever his parents so much as glanced at each other from opposite ends of the long table.

Bruce's cousin, Roger, gave him a sympathetic smile. Bruce stared at his plate. The last thing he wanted was Roger's sympathy. Roger's father had been Henry Patman's brother, but both of Roger's parents were dead now. He had been living with Bruce's family for several months. *Roger's parents were never even married*, Bruce thought. *What can he possibly know about this situation?*

"Bruce," his mother said suddenly, her regal voice sounding loud in the stillness, "what are your plans for spring break?"

Bruce shrugged. "I'm keeping my options open," he said. "Pamela's away, and it's too hot to play tennis . . ."

Bruce's voice drifted off. His mother didn't seem to be listening anyway. Instead, she glared down the long table at Bruce's father, who was studiously eating his prime rib.

Bruce couldn't remember when the house had seemed this quiet. When something clattered in the kitchen, Bruce jumped at the sound as if a firecracker had exploded beneath his chair. Suddenly, he knew he couldn't take another minute of his parents' frosty silences.

"May I be excused?" he asked formally, rising to his feet.

"Uh, me too," Roger said.

Bruce had hoped to get to the wide staircase before Roger had a chance to speak to him, but his cousin was too quick.

"I'm sorry about your parents, Bruce," Roger said in a low voice as the dining-room doors shut behind the boys. "Maybe it's better this way—I mean, they don't seem very happy together."

Bruce scowled at him. "That shows how much you know!"

Roger opened his mouth to reply, but an angry voice from the dining room made both boys turn to stare at the double doors.

"I will not have another pleasant evening destroyed by your sulking," Henry Patman said.

"Sulking?" Marie said, her voice rising. "What else do you expect, when you—"

"I expect you to be open enough to tell me what's got you so angry, instead of giving me this incessant silent treatment."

"Open? You're a fine one to talk about being open, Mr. Henry Wilson Working-Late-Again Patman. I'm not blind, Henry!"

"There you go again, Marie—beating around the

bush. Don't I at least have the right to know what I'm being accused of?"

Bruce was mortified. His parents—the most respected couple in town—were in the dining room, screaming at each other at the top of their lungs. It was bad enough that Bruce had to listen to it. What he really couldn't bear was the thought of Roger and all the servants knowing about his parents' problems, too.

Now both boys plainly heard Marie Patman's usually cultured voice breaking into angry sobs.

"You know very well what I'm accusing you of, Henry," she said, choking on the words. "I'm accusing you of being involved with another woman!"

Chapter 3

Lila watched Jessica's face in the fading sunlight as the girls climbed into Uncle Jimmo's cute, red miniature Jeep. Lila felt awful. Poor Jessica had seemed so excited for the last few days. It was bad enough that she was in for such a surprise when they arrived at Club Paradise. It didn't seem fair for her to lose her luggage, too.

But it's not my fault her suitcase got left in Miami, Lila thought. And nobody had forced Jessica to accept her invitation.

As they drove through a gate marked "Welcome to Paradise," Lila noticed Jessica's heart-shaped face brightening. Jessica's nose was pressed against the window of the Jeep as she gazed out breathlessly— first at a vast, green golf course and then at a row of beautiful beach cabanas silhouetted against a sky that blazed pink with the sunset. Through the palm trees, the Caribbean glimmered, teal in the fading light.

"Look at that!" Jessica said suddenly, her blue eyes wide. She pointed to a huge swimming pool so elaborate that it impressed even Lila. A lush, green "island" in the center of it held a grass-roofed bar, which came to life with tiny lights that twinkled on as the Jeep slowly drove by. Above the bar towered an artificial hill with a sparkling waterfall that cascaded gracefully into the pool.

"Bikini Boutique," Jessica read aloud, pointing to a sign on a small building near the pool. "If that store is still open tonight, I can get a bathing suit there," she said happily. "Then I'll be all prepared for tomorrow morning!"

Lila sighed. She knew it would take a lot more than a bathing suit to prepare Jessica for Monday morning.

Just past the bikini store, Jessica saw colored lights flicking on, like fireflies, over an open-air dance floor. Several couples were already dancing to one of Jessica's favorite songs.

"Hey, Lila!" she said. "Check out the two guys at the last table on the right. Which one do you think is cuter?"

Lila seemed to perk up for the first time that day.

"Definitely the blond one," Lila said authoritatively, "though his friend is pretty gorgeous, too. How old do you think they are—eighteen?"

"At least," Jessica said. "Maybe even nineteen." She pictured herself dancing with the tall, light-haired boy, with those colored lights shining in his sexy, longish hair. She thought wistfully of the slinky red party dress.

Uncle Jimmo swung the Jeep around a bend and through a gate. "And this," he said, gesturing grandly, "is Kiddie Paradise!"

"It's just like Club Paradise," Jessica said, "only everything's in miniature!"

The kiddie swimming pool was smaller than the adult pool. Nearby, children played on a floodlit miniature golf course and sat at tiny tables under the lights of an open-air burger stand.

"It's really kind of cute," Jessica said politely, thinking that Kiddie Paradise might be a novel place to visit—for people who liked children, which she didn't. She thought it was about time to return to the real Club Paradise. She had no way of knowing how late the Bikini Boutique would be open. She wondered if Caribbean bikinis were more exotic than California ones.

But Uncle Jimmo didn't turn the Jeep around. He pulled up in front of a building that looked like a grass-roofed camp cabin.

"Well, here's the staff cabin!" he said brightly. "Your bunks are inside. I hope you don't mind if I don't show you in."

Jessica's stomach turned a sickening somersault. Had she heard him right? *Staff? Bunks? In Kiddie Paradise?*

Suddenly, Jessica was afraid she knew why Lila had been acting so nice to her.

Elizabeth sat cross-legged on the living-room floor Sunday night, surrounded by dusty scrapbooks and photo albums. Beside her sat the Wakefields' golden

34

retriever, Prince Albert, who was panting miserably. Elizabeth's hair fell into her eyes and she swiped it away, leaving a gritty-feeling smudge on her forehead.

At first, Elizabeth had enjoyed poring over the meticulously preserved and dated mementos of her mother's teenage years—photographs, cocktail napkins, and dance cards. But so far, she hadn't learned anything new about who Alice Robertson Wakefield had really been when she was just Alice Robertson.

She selected a thick scrapbook and opened its dusty cover.

"I shouldn't get discouraged," she told herself out loud. "Maybe the next page I turn to will reveal some unusual, romantic story about Mom."

And if it doesn't, she added silently, *I'll just have to be a good investigative journalist and find somewhere else to dig.*

Her mother had more old stuff packed away in the attic. Elizabeth hoped she would find something unexpected there. She decided to ask her mother the next day if she could go through those boxes.

"Lila, I want to know the truth," Jessica said in a horrified whisper. The girls stood in the sandy driveway of the bunkhouse, watching the miniature Jeep drive off toward grown-up land. "What are we doing in Kiddie Paradise?"

"Baby-sitting," Lila mumbled, fiddling with the handle of her suitcase.

"Baby-sitting?"

"Well, not exactly baby-sitting," Lila amended. "We're camp counselors."

35

"Camp counselors in Kiddie Paradise?" Jessica screamed. "Why? How? Why didn't you tell me?"

"Two counselors dropped out at the last minute. My parents volunteered me and a friend."

"A friend?" Jessica asked. "I wouldn't do this to my worst enemy! This was supposed to be the best vacation of my life. I'm in the Caribbean. My clothes are in Miami. And I have to spend the week in Munchkin Land, taking care of little monsters?"

"Look at it from my point of view, Jess. How would you like to be stuck here watching kids all week, all by yourself? This wasn't my idea! I'm here against my will, too."

Jessica shook her head. "Oh, no. It's not the same thing at all. You lied to me! You got me here under false pretenses!"

"You wouldn't have come if I had told you the truth!"

"Of course I wouldn't have come. I'm not an idiot."

Lila smiled weakly and tried to look penitent.

"I'm sorry, Jess," she said with a sniffle. "But you're my very closest friend, and I thought you would understand."

"I can't believe this. You're trying to make *me* feel guilty for being mad at you? Forget it, Lila. I'm the one person who's as good at that as you are. And I'm not going to fall for it!"

"There isn't much you can do except make the best of it," Lila said philosophically. "We may be stuck here with a bunch of screaming brats, but at least we've got each other."

"Oh, no!" Jessica said. "I may be stuck with you, but I'll never forgive you for this. I'm never speaking to you again!"

Amy stood on the Wakefields' doorstep, wiping her forehead with a tissue. It didn't seem right that it could still be so hot, even though it was after eight o'clock in the evening. She had walked only four blocks from her own house, but she felt as hot as she'd ever been in her life. Amy hated to sweat.

Even worse, she hated to study. It wasn't like her to start a paper on Sunday when she had a whole week to work on it. But Barry had left town the day before, Jessica and Lila had left that morning, and Amy was already bored out of her mind.

She rang the Wakefields' doorbell.

"Hi, Liz," she said when Elizabeth answered. She pushed past her into the living room. "Jessica said she would tell you about the paper I'm writing for English class. She said you might be able to help me with my research."

She spoke hesitantly, a little afraid of Elizabeth's reaction. Passing off the twins' relative as her own seemed almost dishonest. Amy didn't think it was a big deal—after all, the woman had been dead for decades! But Elizabeth didn't usually go along with that kind of thing.

"I don't know how much help I'll be on your paper," Elizabeth admitted, following her into the living room. "I mean, it's your family, not mine. But I'd be happy to give you some research tips."

Amy sighed. Jessica apparently hadn't told Elizabeth whom Amy was writing about.

"Sorry about the mess," Elizabeth said, gesturing to the pile of photo albums on the floor. "I've been doing some research for my paper."

Amy had an idea. Maybe she could get Elizabeth to help her research the twins' great-great-grandmother Jessamyn, without knowing she was doing it.

"Why don't you just show me what kinds of papers and things you're going through," Amy suggested. "Maybe that would give me some ideas for where to start."

Prince Albert looked up at the girls lazily. Elizabeth sat down cross-legged on the floor and reached over to scratch his ears. "Sure," she said, "if you think it will help. But I don't have any secret formulas. I'm just looking through these old scrapbooks and photo albums to see if they have anything useful inside. Of course, your first step is knowing the basic facts about the person you've chosen as your subject. Information from resources like these scrapbooks just fills in the blanks. Who are you writing about, anyway?"

"Oh, it's my, uh, my great-great-grandmother. Her name was, um—" Amy stopped, realizing she couldn't say Jessamyn. Prince Albert nudged her leg, wanting to be petted. "Her name was Alberta," she finished quickly, glancing at the dog.

"Here's something interesting," Elizabeth said suddenly, staring at a page of a leather-bound scrapbook.

"It looks like a family tree," Amy said.

"You know, I remember seeing this years ago, when Jessica and I were little kids. My mother drew it herself. Look at the date—she was only thirteen."

The family tree was a quick, informal sketch drawn with colored pencils, but Amy was impressed by the artistic skill it showed. "Wow," she said, "she did this when she was three years younger than us."

"It's funny how all that artistic talent passed right by my generation!" Elizabeth mused. "I can't draw a straight line with a ruler—and Jessica's even worse!"

"A lot of the names have pictures next to them," Amy said. "What do they mean?"

Elizabeth pointed to a name at the top of the tree. "That one with the picture of the little ship is Alice Larson, my great-great-great-grandmother," she explained. "She was sixteen when she left Sweden by herself to travel to America—by ship."

The second row of names caught Amy's attention.

"Elisabeth and Jessamyn?" she asked, pretending to be surprised. "Were they twins, too? And why is there a little horse between their names?"

"Jessamyn was a bareback rider in the circus. And Elisabeth died in a riding accident." She sighed. "Maybe I should be writing a biography about my great-great-grandmother, the circus performer. I'm certainly not learning much about my own mother's early life—except that she could draw horses well!"

Amy gulped. If Elizabeth decided to write about Jessamyn, then Amy would have to rethink her whole paper. Mr. Collins would never believe that they both had great-great-grandmothers who were bareback riders in the circus.

"But your mother's life must be so interesting," Amy protested. "She's such a wonderful person."

Elizabeth smiled. "You're right," she said gratefully. "Although looking through her albums isn't the most exciting thing to do for spring break."

Amy sighed with relief. "I think Jessica and Lila are the only ones who will be having an exciting time this week," she said, leaning against a stack of photo albums. "Some people have all the luck!"

Jessica opened her eyes to see stark, white sunlight pouring across the bed. She blinked, confused.

She had been riding a circus horse, bareback, as the bright sunlight played along the tips of the sapphire waves. The long shawl of her filmy white blouse flowed gracefully behind her.

Then she passed under a sign that screamed in garish pink and aqua: Welcome to Paradise. Hordes of children streamed out of a circus tent with a grass roof, waving miniature golf clubs.

Uncle Jimmo's diabolical laughter echoed over the scene. "I hope the little monsters won't be too much for you!"

Jessica sat up. As the dream faded, the events of the night before came rushing back to her. Around her, four girls slept silently in their bunks. In the bed farthest from Jessica's, a few locks of long, brown hair poked out from beneath the blanket.

Lila.

Jessica narrowed her eyes at her friend's slim form under the blanket. Then she lay back onto her pillow and pulled the sheet over her own face, wishing she could burrow beneath the covers and stay there all week.

"Baby-sitting," she whispered, still incredulous.

Then she nearly fell out of bed. A long, loud scream interrupted her thoughts. It was a whistle blast coming from just outside the bunkhouse— about two feet from Jessica's head.

"Time to get up, girls!" called an annoyingly peppy voice from outside.

A minute later, the owner of the voice stuck her head in the door. The woman was in her twenties, with dark hair cut in a cute bob, and a kindergarten-teacher manner. "Wake up, sleepyheads!" she called brightly. "Orientation begins in one hour!"

Jessica fidgeted on the hard, wooden bench, hoping she would wake up any minute—at home in California, dreaming all of this. *It can't be real,* she told herself. There was just no way that her first day in the Caribbean could be this dull.

OK, maybe the bright blue sky and the gentle, sea-scented breeze are real, she conceded. But she, Jessica Wakefield, was not sitting in an outdoor auditorium at eight o'clock on a Monday morning. And she was certainly not listening to the pixieish brunette perform a song-and-dance routine.

"When the red, red robin comes bob-bob-bobbing along!" sang the woman who had awakened the camp counselors that morning.

Jessica sighed loudly, and the heavyset counselor sitting next to her turned to stare at her. Jessica scowled at her until the girl turned away.

Jessica searched the benches around her. There were eight teenage counselors—five girls and three

41

boys. Unfortunately, even the boys were completely uninteresting—*geeks, every one of them,* Jessica thought, shaking her head sadly.

There was a tall, skinny guy with a pronounced Adam's apple and huge ears. Jessica thought she had heard someone call him Charles. He grinned hopefully at her. Jessica looked away.

The two guys sitting right in front of Jessica were even worse. *Even their names are nerdy,* Jessica thought. Harold and Howard were short and anemic-looking. *They're probably afraid of girls and spend all their time playing video games,* she decided.

Jessica had seen enough of the girls in the last hour to know they were not her type either. Julia, the blonde sitting next to her, had been nasty to Jessica since the moment she woke up—just because Jessica had offered to give her some advice on choosing clothes that would make her look thinner.

Marcy, the tall senior sitting on Jessica's other side, had been a counselor the year before and was now their Bunk Leader. She had been nice enough to find Jessica some official Club Paradise shorts and a top to wear that morning—although the baggy khakis weren't quite Jessica's style. Marcy wasn't really her type. She reminded Jessica of Enid Rollins—too much of an earnest do-gooder.

The other girl, Anne, was very pretty, Jessica had to admit. Anne was tall and thin, with coffee-colored skin and short dark hair. But she was so shy that she'd hardly said a word to Jessica, or anybody else, that morning.

In fact, Lila was the only other person who looked

like somebody Jessica would want to know. But Lila was her archenemy.

"Good morning, Kiddie Kounselors!" the brunette said in her kindergarten-teacher voice after she had, mercifully, finished her song. Jessica squirmed. "Welcome to Paradise! I'm the Kounselor Koordinator, Trixie Nash, and I'm here to help you!"

"Trixie the Pixie," Jessica said under her breath. She didn't think she'd ever seen such a peppy human being in her entire life.

"First, I'll give you a preview of what your next five days will be like," Trixie said. "Every counselor will be assigned a group of five or six children of about the same age," Trixie explained. "We call them our HLKs, for Happy Little Kampers. The HLKs live in bunkhouses just like yours, here in Kiddie Paradise, while their parents are enjoying themselves with the other adults at Grown-up Paradise."

Jessica felt her boredom turning to despair. She thought of the beachfront cabanas she'd seen at sunset the evening before. She sighed miserably, ignoring a pointed stare from Julia.

"You'll be leading your little charges in a variety of activities," Trixie said, "including finger painting, water sports, and games. The rotation schedule for each day will be posted at breakfast. You will eat all of your meals with the children, at the Kiddie Kabana—except for breakfast, which will be here in this meeting area, which is called the Kiddie Korral."

Jessica glared daggers at the back of Lila's head three rows in front of her. It was bad enough that she

43

had been brought here, under false pretenses, to baby-sit a bunch of little monsters. And the hard bunk, baggy khaki shorts, and cold shower hadn't done anything to help her mood. But it kept getting worse! From the way Trixie emphasized all the Kiddie Paradise names, Jessica could practically hear all the *K*'s. *How Kute*, she thought.

"That song about the red robin is one that I always like to start Monday mornings with," Trixie continued. "But beginning tomorrow morning, the entertainment will be your responsibility!"

Jessica gulped. This sounded ominous.

"This is one of the best parts of your day as a camp counselor!" Trixie gushed. "Every counselor will prepare a different song, dance, or similar routine to perform each day for the next three mornings. Your acts will be presented after breakfast on Tuesday, Wednesday, and Thursday, to welcome our guests. You can use any resources you have available. You can even team up and do something together. The only rule is that every counselor must participate. The purpose is to remind the children of how pleased we are to have them with us. Remember, the children are our customers. We're here to see that they are Happy Little Kampers!"

They'll be happy kampers, all right, Jessica thought. *The little monsters will be thrilled to see us making fools of ourselves every morning.*

Jessica noticed with satisfaction that Lila's shoulders were drooping as miserably as her own.

"But it gets even better," Trixie promised, smiling broadly.

"Even better than *this*?" Jessica whispered sarcastically.

"As camp counselors, you are in charge of the end-of-the-week entertainment for the kids and their parents. All the counselors work together to organize and perform in a talent show on Friday evening! You'll have to be very resourceful, coming up with ideas and costumes and materials. It will be lots of fun!"

Jessica pinched herself on the arm, hard. Her fingernails left white crescents on her tanned skin. Obviously, she was not dreaming. She was stuck here, baby-sitting, all week. And she would have to embarrass herself in front of everyone on Friday.

"It isn't right," Bruce whispered as he paced in the downstairs hallway of the Patman mansion Monday morning. He banged a fist, painfully, against his thigh. *So what if they argue now and then?* he asked himself. *That's no reason to throw away twenty years of being a family!*

It had been three days since Bruce's parents had announced their separation. Mr. Patman had told Bruce he would get used to the idea, but Bruce wasn't getting used to it. Not one bit.

As for his father having an affair, Bruce didn't believe it for an instant. Henry Patman was too much the pillar-of-the-community type to cheat on his wife. His mother had just been upset last night; she had gotten emotional and made wild accusations. *Women are like that,* Bruce thought. It was up to Bruce's father to buy her some flowers, apologize for getting

45

angry, and convince her that she was the only woman for him.

Bruce couldn't believe his parents would be so selfish. *They have no right to do this to me! They probably never even considered the effect a divorce would have on my life!*

Well, Bruce wasn't going to take it lying down. He was going to march into his father's den and say exactly what he thought of this ridiculous idea—as soon as he mustered up the nerve.

Bruce never would have admitted it to anyone, but he had always been a little intimidated by his father. In fact, Henry Patman's ability to intimidate people was one of the things Bruce admired about him. He wanted to be just like his father someday—a rich, powerful, successful businessman. Somebody to be envied, respected, and feared. A man who was in control of his destiny.

Bruce shook his head. If Henry Patman were really in control, he'd never have allowed his relationship with his wife to reach this point.

"How could you let this happen?" Bruce said under his breath, staring at the door to his father's den.

The door was ajar. Bruce put his hand on it and was about to push it open. He stopped when he heard a voice inside. His father was on the phone, Bruce realized, and it sounded like business. He would have to wait for the call to end. Henry Patman never liked to be interrupted when he was talking about business.

"I'm so glad you've agreed to take this design-consultant job," he was saying. "Those jokers we hired in Chicago are hopelessly off schedule, but with you heading the team, I'm sure we can get them back on track."

Bruce tapped his foot impatiently. He knew his father had spent hours this weekend working with a local design consultant on a big project for the new Chicago plant. He remembered hearing his father talk about spending a lot more time with the consultant in the next few weeks.

He ought to be spending more time trying to fix things here at home, Bruce thought resentfully, *instead of worrying about a plant that's two thousand miles away.*

"You think that's what I'm doing?" Henry Patman was saying into the phone, an unfamiliar note in his voice. Bruce blinked. His father sounded *playful*! That wasn't Henry Patman's usual business style. It was odd. Somebody who was separating from his wife was supposed to sound upset.

His father continued happily. "You think swooping into Chicago this week with no warning is just another one of my grand gestures?" he asked into the phone, laughing. "Well, maybe it is. But you have to admit—a grand gesture can be very useful now and then. It worked on you, didn't it?"

Bruce was mystified. Henry Patman, never one to mix business with pleasure, was laughing his head off with a consultant. He was acting like a fraternity boy.

Maybe this thing with Mom is really sending him off the deep end, Bruce reflected.

Now Henry was chuckling again, apparently in response to something the consultant was saying.

"But you should have seen the look on the florist's face," he replied a moment later, "when I told her I wanted to send you every red rose in Southern California!"

Bruce shook his head. He must have heard his father wrong. It was the only explanation.

Mr. Patman lowered his voice, and Bruce had to strain his ears to catch the next line.

"And I wished I could have seen the look on your face, Alice," he said seriously, "when you received those roses."

Bruce's mouth dropped open. He knew only one local design consultant named Alice.

With a sickening feeling, he remembered his mother's tearful accusation the night before. Suddenly, Bruce's knees felt weak.

His father *was* having an affair—with Alice Wakefield.

Chapter 4

"Children, this is your Kiddie Kounselor, Jessica Wakefield," Trixie said to six bored-looking children after Monday's orientation. "Jessica, your five- and six-year-olds."

All around Jessica in the Kiddie Korral, other staff members were introducing Kiddie Kounselors to their Happy Little Kampers.

"The boys are Gerry Pat, Lorenzo, and Bobby," Trixie said, pointing them out to Jessica. "Gerry Pat is really Gerald Patrick, but they call him Gerry Pat for short. Isn't that cute?"

Jessica eyed the chubby redheaded boy warily. Gerry Pat was staring at her with his green eyes narrowed and a thoughtful look on his face. *He's probably already imagining how I'm going to make a fool out of myself in this stupid morning-welcome routine tomorrow,* Jessica thought.

"I don't like it here," the tallest boy said in a

49

sullen voice, interrupting Jessica's thoughts. "And I don't like you, either."

Trixie laughed. "Lorenzo is such a little kidder!" she exclaimed. "Lorenzo and Gerry Pat are six years old. Bobby's five. Bobby, take your finger out of your mouth and say hello to Jessica."

The skinny, blond child removed the grubby finger from his mouth. Then he leaned forward and wiped it on the hem of Jessica's shorts. Jessica almost screamed.

"The girls are Karen, Maria, and Suzy," Trixie continued. "Suzy is a bit younger than the other children in your group—she's not quite five years old—but her parents wanted her to be with her big sister, Karen, who's six. I'm sure you're all going to get along famously!"

Curly-haired Maria was probably the cutest one in the bunch, Jessica decided, despite having what looked like sticky grape jelly smeared on her face. The round-faced five-year-old shyly placed a hand in Jessica's. Jessica realized that the little hand was as sticky as the girl's face.

Trixie left to introduce Julia to her seven- and eight-year-olds. Suzy stared up at Jessica with a mean glint in her dark eyes.

"I'm Suzy," said the chubby little girl. "And I have to go to the bathroom."

"She always has to go to the bathroom," said the tallest girl, tossing her dark, straight hair with an air of importance. "That's what Mommy says."

"She does not say that!"

Karen stuck out her tongue, and Jessica stared at

the six-year-old, disgusted but impressed, as the girl's tongue curled upward until it touched the tip of her nose.

"How did she do that?" asked red-haired Gerry Pat in a stage whisper, poking Lorenzo in the ribs.

Lorenzo opened his mouth as if he were about to lick his own nose, but instead, grabbed Gerry Pat's arm and bit it.

"Don't you ever poke me!" Lorenzo commanded.

Gerry Pat began crying. Bobby gave Maria's dirty blond curls a swift yank.

"Stop it!" Jessica said angrily. The children ignored her.

"Stop it!" Karen commanded, with no better results. "You're acting like children!"

"And you're bossy!" Lorenzo said, turning on Karen. "I'm going to bite you, too!"

Karen screamed. Gerry Pat tried to touch his nose with his tongue. Maria hid behind Jessica's baggy shorts, her huge blue eyes wet with tears.

Bobby tugged on Jessica's arm. "I know some magic tricks!" he boasted. "Want to see some magic tricks?"

"Not now!" Jessica screamed. "Shut up, all of you!"

All six children became quiet suddenly, but not in response to Jessica's order. They turned to gape as Lila walked by with her nose in the air. In a straight line behind her, six obedient kindergartners waddled like baby geese, singing in unison, "Row, row, row your yacht . . ."

Naturally, thought Jessica.

"Wimps!" Karen said, glaring at the well-behaved children.

Jessica's charges began snickering at Lila and her kids, and Jessica thought she saw Lorenzo throw a pebble at Lila. She fought the urge to run after her ex–best friend and smear her grape-jelly-covered hand all over Lila's sparkling white shirt.

"I still have to go to the bathroom!" warned Suzy.

Enid shook a french fry across the table at the Dairi Burger after Monday's matinee. "But, Liz, it would have been wrong for her to break up her marriage to go back to an old boyfriend."

Olivia, sitting next to Enid, had to admit that she was right. People should take their marriage vows seriously.

"Wrong?" Elizabeth asked. "It would have been even more wrong for her to deny her one true love!"

Elizabeth's argument made sense, too, Olivia realized. *After all, what was the sense of staying in a marriage when you were really in love with somebody else?*

Olivia chuckled under her breath. She always thought of Elizabeth and Enid as mild-mannered, reasonable types who took the time to see every side of a question. Olivia was the passionate, artistic one of the three. But her friends' discussion about *Casablanca* was getting pretty heated—and it had nothing to do with the ninety-five-degree temperature outside. "It's a good thing this place is air-conditioned," she said. "The way you two are going at it—"

"Normally, Enid, I'd agree with you about not wanting to break up a marriage," Elizabeth interrupted. "In most cases, it *is* wrong to have an affair and wreck a family. But this is different!"

Olivia opened her mouth to respond.

"No, Liz, it isn't different!" Enid broke in. "Ingrid Bergman was happily married. Why should she have thrown all that away? Her marriage had no problems until she happened to run into her old flame in Casablanca."

Olivia had to admit again that Enid had a valid point. She spoke out of the side of her mouth in a Bogart impersonation. " 'Of all the gin joints in all the towns—' "

"Bergman may not have had any actual problems with her husband," Elizabeth broke in, "but she didn't really love him—not the way she loved Bogie. She only stayed with her husband out of loyalty. She should have followed her heart instead."

"I guess you're right, Liz," Olivia managed to put in. "On the other hand, she and Bogart only had a short time together in Paris, and that was years ago. How would she know that the relationship—"

"Of course she would know!" Elizabeth insisted staunchly. "There is one true love for every person, and Humphrey Bogart was definitely Ingrid Bergman's—"

"There you are, Wakefield!" yelled an angry Bruce Patman, storming across the room. He crossed his arms in front of his chest and glowered at Elizabeth. "Everything that's wrong is all your family's fault!"

"Whoa, Bruce!" Enid said with a nervous laugh. "I can think of at least three or four world problems that the Wakefields had nothing to do with."

Bruce turned on her. "Mind your own business, egghead!"

Elizabeth stood up and crossed her own arms. To

Olivia's imaginative eye, pretty, blond Elizabeth looked as if she was about to breathe fire—which, Olivia had to admit, might not be hard to do in this weather.

Now Bruce is really going to catch it, Olivia realized. The one thing Elizabeth was never mild-mannered about was an insult to her friends or family.

"Bruce Patman!" Elizabeth said. "I'm sick of the way you treat everyone. Why don't you go count your money or something?"

Olivia caught Enid's eye and grinned. That was telling him.

"Well, excuse me, Miss Perfect," Bruce countered. "And I'm sick of your Goody Two Shoes act! You think that you and your rotten little family are so much more *moral* than everybody else in town. I guess we all know now that it's just not true!"

"You leave my family out of this!"

"Oh, I forgot," Bruce said sarcastically. "You're the fine, upstanding twin. You're too pure and innocent to know what your two-timing mother is doing. How long has it been going on, Liz? How long have you been laughing at me behind my back?"

"Were you born this way, Bruce?" Olivia asked, rising to her feet. "Or were you dropped on your head as a child?"

"Bruce," Elizabeth said in a controlled voice. "I don't have the faintest idea what you're talking about. Just what are you accusing me of? What right do you have to criticize my mother?"

"I have every right—when your mother is breaking up my parents' marriage!"

Elizabeth stared at him, speechless. Olivia almost laughed out loud.

"Bruce," Elizabeth said incredulously. "I know you're upset about your parents' separation, but you're not making any sense. What could my mother possibly have to do with your parents' marriage?"

Bruce's ice-blue eyes widened with realization, and he laughed coldly. "You're actually serious, Liz," he said. "You really don't know anything about it, do you?"

"The only thing I know is that this conversation has gone on long enough," Elizabeth said. "If you're not going to say anything coherent, go talk to yourself in a corner somewhere, so we can get on with our own discussion."

She sat down in the booth as if to end the conversation.

"Come on, Liz!" Bruce said, sliding into the booth next to Elizabeth. "This affects you as much as it affects me. Haven't you noticed how much time your mother is spending with my father lately? They're having an affair!"

"That's ridiculous! They're spending time together because your father hired her to work on a project in his Chicago plant. It's just business! Whatever gave you the crackpot idea that—"

"That's right, Liz. Bury your head in the sand while he sends her flowers and makes their travel plans. You just go on believing everything is hunky-dory. But that won't change the fact that your mother is breaking up my family!"

"Bruce," Elizabeth began, "I'm only going to say

this once. My mother is in love with my father. She has never loved any other man, and she never will."

"Liz, I heard them on the phone this morning. He said he sent her every red rose in Southern California!"

"Bruce, I can tell that reality is not your strong point today, but don't you think I'd have noticed if a hundred dozen roses were delivered to my door?"

"You are so naive," Bruce said. "She's too slick to let him send them to the house. I bet he sent them to her office."

"Bruce, I'm not going to listen to any more of this," Elizabeth yelled. "Take your delusions and get out of here!"

Bruce scowled and jumped to his feet. Olivia watched him stalk across the restaurant. As he kicked open the door, white-hot sunlight spilled inside, distorting Bruce's usually handsome features for an instant before the door closed behind him. Olivia turned back to her friends. Elizabeth seemed close to tears.

"Liz, you're shaking," Olivia said.

"It's all right, Elizabeth," Enid said. "You handled him well. I was proud of you."

"But why would he suggest such a thing—and in front of everybody?" Elizabeth asked.

"Everyone knows Bruce is a jerk," Olivia said. "Don't pay any attention to his ranting and raving. Nobody else will."

"But an affair?" Elizabeth said. "Between my mother and Mr. Patman? It's ludicrous! My parents have had their troubles, like anyone else, but they're more in love now than ever!"

"We know that, Liz," Enid said. "But Bruce is probably very angry at his parents—he's just trying to make himself feel better by blaming somebody else."

"That's it exactly," Olivia agreed. "Besides, no woman in her right mind would have an affair with somebody who's just an older version of Bruce!"

"They're not having an affair!" Elizabeth said ardently. "And I'll prove it to Bruce!"

"You don't have to prove anything to that jerk," Enid said.

"I don't have to, but I will," Elizabeth vowed. "Somehow, I'm going to prove to Bruce that the only thing between his father and my mother is a little unfinished business."

Lila stood over a table in the Kiddie Kabana, where her six kindergarten-age HLKs happily made puppets out of tube socks.

It was late Monday afternoon, and the children were being quiet and obedient—*naturally,* Lila thought. They wouldn't dare act like those screaming monsters Jessica was saddled with. Lila had a problem to think through, and she couldn't concentrate if a half-dozen brats were asking her questions all the time. Lila had decided long ago that children should be seen and not heard. It was all a matter of knowing how to handle them.

With the children busy, Lila was free to think about a more important topic—boys.

Ever since her classmate John Pfeifer had tried to rape her a few months earlier, Lila had been cautious about dating. But now she was feeling confident and strong again. A Caribbean vacation was the perfect time for testing the limits—even for going a little bit crazy. Within reason, of course. A brief romantic fling in a lush, tropical setting was just what Lila needed to assure herself that she was back in control—in control of her emotions and her relationships.

Her current problem was choosing the perfect boy. She had been scanning the island carefully since her arrival the night before. Club Paradise was full of great-looking guys, but Lila only had a week. Of the boys she had seen, there weren't a lot of candidates. All three of the male counselors were complete drips.

In fact, Lila had seen only two boys who were worth considering. Dark-haired Larry was the lifeguard at the Kiddie Paradise pool. She'd met him only briefly; he was cute and seemed to have a sense of humor. The other candidate interested her more. He was the tall, blond, and incredibly gorgeous guy she and Jessica had noticed from the window of Uncle Jimmo's Jeep. He was not only the best-looking boy Lila had seen on the island, he was the best-looking boy Lila had ever seen, period.

Unfortunately, Lila didn't even know his name. Through discreet eavesdropping, she had learned that Club Paradise had an attractive blond windsurfing instructor. Lila couldn't claim to be an expert in Club Paradise personnel, but she did know a lot about handsome boys. And the only person she'd seen who fit that description was the blond boy at the disco. Lila trusted her intuition in such matters. She was willing to bet the attractive blond boy was the windsurfing instructor.

So what's the next step? she asked herself. She could give Uncle Jimmo's office a call and ask who to talk to for some windsurfing tips.

"No," she said under her breath. "Too obvious. I need something more discreet."

"Lila," one of her five-year-olds piped up, "I'm finished with my sock puppet. What can I do now?"

Lila turned and stared at the little boy thoughtfully. *Kids notice everything,* she thought. And that pixieish Trixie person had said that a lot of these children came back to Club Paradise with their families every year.

"Bartholomew," she asked him, "have you been to this place before?"

"Yup," said the blond boy. "Lots of times." He began to count on his fingers. "One, two, three, six times!"

"What do your parents do when they're here?"

"Daddy plays golf—where he hits a ball into a pond," he explained. "And Mommy plays games in the ocean."

Lila tried not to sound impatient. "What kinds of games does she play? Does she go boating and snorkeling and windsurfing?"

Bartholomew nodded. "She says she likes windsurfing best. She says she windsurfs with a fox. I know about foxes. They're red squirrels with pointy faces and bushy tails. But I never saw a fox in the ocean. Did you?"

"Sure," Lila said, sure that she was getting close to an answer. "Lots of times. Is there a boy who helps your mother windsurf? Did she tell you his name?"

"Not a boy," Bartholomew said knowingly. "A man. He's forty years old. Or maybe even nineteen. She says his name is Mick."

"Forty or nineteen, huh?" Lila asked. Obviously, Bartholomew was better at sock puppets than at counting.

A six-year-old girl with curly black hair stood up. "I know the windsurfing man," she said. "My mommy likes to windsurf. She said she'd follow Mick Myers off a cliff if he asked her to. Why would he ask her to go off a cliff?"

Lila smiled, convinced that Mick Myers was the boy she had in mind. "I think it's a figure of speech, Heidi. Have you seen Mick Myers? Do you know where I can find him?"

"I see Mick sometimes," Heidi said. "His friend is Larry the Lifeguard. Sometimes they eat dinner in the Kiddie Banana."

Lila was mystified. "Kiddie Banana?" she asked.

Heidi looked at her as if she thought Lila were stupid. "Where we are now."

Lila chuckled. *Of course. Heidi means Kiddie Kabana.* And dinner was less than an hour away. If she was lucky, gorgeous, blond Mick Myers would be there to have dinner with Larry.

Heidi shook her head. "Grown-ups are weird."

"Thanks for being such good friends, both of you," Elizabeth said warmly as Enid stopped her mother's blue hatchback in front of the Wakefield house. "I guess I went kind of crazy at the Dairi Burger."

60

"No way!" Enid objected. "Bruce was the one who went crazy."

"Extremely crazy," Olivia agreed. "Just try to forget about him. Concentrate on Katharine Hepburn and Spencer Tracy instead."

"That's right," Elizabeth remembered. "Tomorrow's movie is *Adam's Rib*. I can't wait."

"Enid drove today, so it's my turn tomorrow," Olivia said as Elizabeth jumped out. "I'll pick you up at one o'clock."

After her friends drove away, Elizabeth took a deep breath and walked up the front path. As she approached the pretty, split-level home, the front door swung open and her mother hurried out, carrying a garment bag.

"Oh, Liz," she said, "I'm glad you're home, sweetheart, so I can kiss you good-bye."

"Goodbye?"

"I've called your father at the office, and I left a note in the kitchen for you. I have to go to Chicago for this project. It's probably for only a couple of days, but I won't be sure until I get there. I know it's sudden, but there's a meeting first thing in the morning, so we're leaving now. Can you handle dinner for you and your father? I left salad fixings in the fridge."

"Of course. But Chicago? Who are you going with?"

Alice laid the garment bag across the backseat of her car. "Hank Patman."

The sun was sinking red in the western sky as Elizabeth watched her mother's car drive off. Elizabeth's heart sank, too.

Her mother was going to Chicago with Bruce

Patman's father? Surely it was just a coincidence. As her mother had said, they were working on an important business project.

The phone was ringing as Elizabeth trudged into the house.

"What did I tell you?" said Bruce Patman's sneering voice. "My father just left for his trip to Chicago. He says he's meeting your mother at the airport. Now do you believe your mother is the reason my parents are splitting up?"

"Don't jump to conclusions, Bruce," she said. "You know our parents are business associates. They have to straighten out the problems at Patman Canning's Chicago plant."

"Grow up, Liz," Bruce scoffed. "It's time you faced facts. They're having an affair. Your mother is a no-good home-wrecker!"

Elizabeth opened her mouth to reply, but Bruce had already hung up on her.

Numbly, she dialed Enid's number.

"I'm so glad you're home, Enid," she said.

"I just walked through the door," Enid said. "What's wrong, Liz? You sound—stunned."

"That's a good word for it. I was so sure at the Dairi Burger that Bruce was nuts. But now there's this trip to Chicago, and I don't know what to think, and Bruce blames—"

"Hold on, Liz. Tell me what happened."

"My mother just left for Chicago with Bruce's father."

"So? They're business associates, right? So a business trip just happened to come up right after Bruce assaulted us with that ridiculous story. Everyone knows Bruce is paranoid. But you shouldn't be jumping to wild conclusions about it, too."

Elizabeth took a deep breath. "That's just what I told Bruce when he called," she said in a soft voice.

"And you were absolutely right. As a journalist, you get all the facts before you try to tell the story, right?"

"You're right, Enid. I shouldn't be taking Bruce's word for anything. Well, this journalist is going to do some investigating before reaching any more conclusions."

As Elizabeth hung up the phone, she remembered that she never got the chance to ask her mother about going through her old boxes up in the attic.

"Maybe it's just as well Mom doesn't know," she said aloud.

"Lorenzo, you get back here this instant!" Jessica yelled at dinnertime Monday as she entered the Kiddie Kabana open-air restaurant. Her group of Happy Little Monsters, as she had come to think of them, swarmed around her.

Lorenzo put his hands on his hips. "You're mean, and I don't have to listen to you!"

Pudgy little Gerry Pat glanced at the taller boy for approval and then blew a raspberry at Jessica. "I don't have to listen to you, either!" he declared. "I'm going to listen to my own self!"

Lorenzo glared at him. "I'll bite you, Gerry Pat!" he warned.

Gerry Pat's green eyes got big. "I'm going to listen

to him!" he amended, pointing at Lorenzo. "He's my boss now."

"But I'm the oldest!" Karen objected.

"You're a girl!" Lorenzo protested.

"Well, I'm older than any of you!" Jessica said, stamping her foot. "And I want all of you to get into that line to get your dinners. Hurry up, or all the food will be gone."

Suzy started crying.

"Very good, Wakefield!" Julia said sarcastically as she walked by. "Throw a temper tantrum—that's the way to control kids. Did you learn that in your fancy California high school?"

Jessica glared at her, speechless. Julia laughed and stomped off to where her own group of campers was waiting.

"Do you want to see my magic tricks?" Bobby asked.

Jessica rolled her eyes. "The only magic trick I want to see right now is all of you brats disappearing!" she said. "I don't need this aggravation. I'm going to sit over there and relax. If you spoiled little monsters want to eat, you'll get in that cafeteria line. If you don't want to eat, fine. I don't care!"

Jessica turned her back on the children, crossing her arms at her chest. A moment later, she felt a tug on the hem of her now-filthy khaki shorts.

Little Maria was standing there, with an angelic look on her face. "Would you please hold this for me, Jessica, while I get my dinner?" she asked sweetly, sticking out her fist.

As exasperated as Jessica was, she found the little

girl's smile hard to resist—especially since Maria was the only one of the bunch who had been at all pleasant to her. She held out her hand to the five-year-old, who carefully deposited her treasure into it—a wad of chewed-up bubble gum.

"You disgusting little urchin!" Jessica screamed.

Maria scurried off to join the rest of the group in the cafeteria line. They were cheerfully hitting the other campers with their trays.

Jessica shook her head and walked to the nearest empty table. She was supposed to accompany the kids to get their food, but they seemed more than capable of looking out for themselves. Besides, she wasn't hungry. She collapsed into a chair and glanced around to see how the other counselors were faring.

She narrowed her blue-green eyes. Lila stood near a table where six darling children sat eating, napkins tucked neatly into their collars. Jessica shook her head. It was unnatural.

"I bet they're running you ragged," said a voice. For the first time, Jessica noticed a counselor sitting at the other end of the table she'd chosen. It was Anne, the tall, quiet girl.

"Where are your kids?" Jessica asked.

"I've got three- and four-year-olds," Anne explained. "They get a special little-kids orientation this evening, with their parents. So they're off my hands for dinner, just for tonight."

"I wish I could get mine off my hands," Jessica said, staring morosely across the Kiddie Kabana at Lila and her charges. "It's just not fair."

Anne followed her gaze. "I see what you mean,"

she said with a chuckle. "Lila seems to be baby-sitting the Von Trapp Family Singers."

Jessica scowled. "And I'm stuck with the Addams Family!

Anne laughed, and Jessica threw her a dark look. *Anne is about as annoying as Lila,* she thought. *She obviously doesn't understand the seriousness of my situation.*

"Lila doesn't even have to watch her kids," Jessica complained. "Look at that! They're still perfect little angels, even though she's got her back to them, talking to some guy."

Jessica did a double take. Lila wasn't talking to just some guy. Lila was talking to the most gorgeous guy Jessica had ever seen. It looked like the boy she and Lila had noticed at the disco the night before, from the window of Uncle Jimmo's Jeep. He was tall and lean, with broad shoulders, an incredible tan, and long blond hair that shone like silk.

"I've got to go," Anne said. "I'm meeting my kids at the Korral soon, and I'd like to change out of these grubby clothes."

Jessica hardly noticed her leave. She was still watching the golden-haired boy who seemed to be hanging on Lila's every word.

"Hey, Jessica!" Marcy said, walking by with a look of vague disapproval. "What have you done with your Happy Little Kampers?"

Marcy's HLKs—nine- and ten-year-olds, Jessica guessed—were straggling behind the tall girl in a ragged line, carrying their dinner trays. Jessica was relieved to see them arguing mildly among them-

66

selves and occasionally trying to trip one another. At least they weren't perfect, like Lila's charges.

"Oh, they're still in the cafeteria line," Jessica said. "I just had to sit down for a minute before I died of exhaustion."

"I don't blame you," Marcy said with a laugh. "You seem to have gotten stuck with the Brat Pack this week. There's one in every group of campers. Don't feel too bad," she added. "They're just normal kids—far from perfect!"

"They're far from normal," Jessica said. "Everyone else's kids are better behaved than my little brats!"

"So were Attila and the Huns," Marcy quipped. "Actually, I've been meaning to warn you. I've got the big sister of one of your little boys. Kelly keeps telling the other kids what a brat her brother is." Marcy laughed. "She calls him The Pudge!"

Jessica stored the information away for future use.

"Anyhow," Marcy continued, "Kelly says her little brother will do anything—no matter how stupid—if a bigger boy eggs him on. I'd watch Gerry Pat, with that Lorenzo of yours. Looks like a recipe for trouble."

"Don't you think I know that?" Jessica snapped. The last thing she needed was some big-shot counselor telling her what she already knew about her own little brats. Then she stopped herself. Marcy was an old-timer here; she might know the identity of Lila's new, blond friend.

"Sorry," Jessica said with a weak smile. "It's not your fault the little darlings are driving me crazy. I just wish I had a crew like Lila's." She gestured across

67

the room. "Speaking of Lila—who's the guy she's talking to?"

"Mick? He's the windsurfing instructor here. He looks like a god, but watch it—he's got an ego to match. My advice is to stay away from Mick Myers, Jessica. And warn your friend, Lila, to do the same."

"She's not my friend!"

"Sorry," Marcy said. "I just assumed, since you two arrived together . . . Anyhow, Mick can be a real jerk to women. Believe me, I know from personal experience! Not that you'll have much time to worry about boys this week—at least, boys over the age of six." She pointed toward the cafeteria line.

Jessica sighed hopelessly. Her kids had just emerged with their trays. Now they were standing in a circle, cheering, as Bobby sculpted a white beard onto Maria's face—in mashed potatoes.

Chapter 5

"Are you sure you're all right, honey?" Ned Wake-field asked, staring thoughtfully across the kitchen table at Elizabeth.

Just my luck, Elizabeth thought. *Dad would choose tonight to become Mr. Sensitive.*

"Oh, I'm just great!" she said quickly. "Why wouldn't I be? After all, it's the first day of spring break. Would you like some more potato salad?"

"Sure," he said, holding out his plate. "But you really do seem a little tense, Liz."

"It's the heat," Elizabeth said. "It has everyone a little uptight." Elizabeth resolved to act more cheerful. It would never do for her father to find out about Bruce's allegations. *But maybe he can help me investigate Bruce's charges, without even knowing it,* she thought. "You know, I was planning to interview Mom tonight for my English paper—I want to get some details about her life before she got married.

But I'm kind of stuck until I can get some more information. Can you answer a few questions?"

Mr. Wakefield shrugged. "I'll try," he said. "But I don't think there's that much to tell."

"Well, I know you met at college, but I don't know any of the details," Elizabeth said.

"Actually, it's kind of a dramatic story."

Elizabeth's eyes widened. "What happened?" she asked eagerly.

"We were both undergraduates at the College of Southern California," Mr. Wakefield said. "Alice was very much involved in the protest marches and sit-ins that were going on at the time. I guess I was involved, too, but in a backstage sort of way—giving people legal advice and all that. Your mother was one of the real movers and shakers."

"How well did you know her before you started dating?"

"I'd seen her around. And of course I was attracted to her. Who wouldn't be? But she was so popular that she was always surrounded by people. I doubt she even knew I was alive until spring break. There was this big beach party—"

"And you asked her to the party?" Elizabeth interrupted.

"No," said Mr. Wakefield. "I wasn't going to the party. I was what you kids would have called a nerd—or is that a geek?—you know, pre-law, and very serious about it."

He paused thoughtfully and sipped his iced tea.

"So what happened?" Elizabeth prodded.

"I was walking along the beach, minding my own

business. In the distance, I could hear music from the beach party. Then I noticed a blond girl walking into the water. She swam out pretty far from shore, but she was a strong swimmer, so I wasn't concerned. As she turned back toward the beach, she got caught in an undertow. I could see she was in trouble, cramping up. Then her head disappeared under the waves."

"What did you do?"

"I was in the water in an instant. It happened so fast that I hardly remember pulling her out of the ocean. Then we were both dripping on the sand. She was unconscious, and a crowd was gathering. But she was breathing. I could tell she was going to be fine."

"I can't believe you never told me about that!" Elizabeth said, trying to sound more interested than she felt. Normally, she would have been excited about the story. But now, she was more concerned with Bruce's allegations than with her English paper. And the story didn't help her investigation into her mother's relationship with Henry Patman.

Then she had another thought. "So if you weren't Mom's date at that beach party, who was? Why wasn't he the one to save her?"

Mr. Wakefield shrugged. "I don't remember," he said, almost too cheerfully. "Does it matter?"

"I guess not," Elizabeth said. "Did you start dating her soon after that?"

"Not too long afterward," he said noncommittally.

"You said she was always surrounded by other guys," Elizabeth said. "I guess you had a lot of competition."

Her father looked at her strangely. "Just what kind of paper are you writing? Is this one of those kiss-and-tell things?"

Elizabeth laughed, and he joined in.

"Anyhow," he continued, "I said she was always surrounded by other *people*. I guess there must have been other guys. But the best man won out!"

Elizabeth forced herself to smile. "How long after you met her did you know she was the person you wanted to marry?"

"Oh, quite a long time," Mr. Wakefield said. "It was at least one minute—maybe even two. Luckily, it all worked out in the end." He pushed his plate away. "Do you want dessert? I think there's double-chocolate ice cream in the freezer."

Elizabeth smiled, but she was feeling discouraged. Her father was no help at all.

"Do you know if Mom has any old boxes of stuff up in the attic I could look through?" she asked. "I've already gone through the scrapbooks and photo albums down here."

He scratched his head. "I'm not sure, honey. I don't think she'd mind you digging around to see what you can find. But it's probably a hundred and twenty-five degrees up there."

Elizabeth grimaced. "On second thought, maybe tomorrow morning would be better. Now what were you saying about double-chocolate ice cream?"

"You were supposed to do a song or dance," Julia whispered as the halfhearted applause trailed off Tuesday morning. Jessica scowled and sat down next to the other counselor on one of the hard benches of the Kiddie Korral.

"Trixie said we could do a song, dance, or similar routine," Jessica whispered angrily. She was still blushing from the humiliation of performing in front of the group. "A cheer is a similar routine."

Jessica felt a squeeze on her shoulder and turned to face Charles Grogan, the tall, skinny counselor.

"You did great, Jessica," he said, grinning broadly. "You're a wonderful cheerleader."

"Thanks," Jessica said coldly. "But nobody else seems to think so."

She turned away, pretending to be absorbed in the modern-dance routine that Marcy was beginning onstage. She was glad that the music was loud enough so that nobody but Julia could have heard Charles's praise. She didn't want it to get around that there was anything between her and a dork like him. Still, she was pleased to notice a jealous gleam in Julia's hard gray eyes.

"Cheerleading is stupid," Julia whispered a minute later. "And you shouldn't have yanked out all those palm fronds to tie together for pompons. How do you know that they're not an endangered species?"

"You're going to be an endangered species if you don't shut up and leave me alone!" Jessica hissed, a little louder. "What else was I supposed to use for pompons? Those trees aren't endangered. They're growing all over this island."

She turned back to Charles, knowing it would infuriate Julia. "Don't you agree, Charles?"

"Yes, Jessica, I think you're right," Charles replied

seriously. "But you shouldn't be pulling palm fronds all by yourself. The next time you need help, just ask me."

"Why, thank you, Charles," Jessica said graciously, with a sidelong look at Julia. *Charles might have his uses, after all,* she thought.

"Cheerleaders have pompons for brains," Julia whispered, low enough so that Charles wouldn't hear. "Only girls with no other talent would be caught dead cheerleading."

"You're just jealous, because you're too fat to be a cheerleader and to have boys notice you! But I suppose you have tons of talent to show off this morning."

"As a matter of fact, I do," Julia said, rising to her feet.

"Fat chance," Jessica said pointedly.

"See for yourself," Julia said. "I'm on next."

She got up and flounced down the aisle to the stage.

When the plump blonde began to sing "Wilkommen" from *Cabaret*, Jessica wanted to sink into the floor. Julia had a terrific alto voice.

The only thing that would make it possible for her to survive the rest of the morning, Jessica decided, was seeing Lila's performance. Jessica knew that Lila had no talent whatsoever, except for hosting parties and buying clothes—and lying to her friends.

"Thank you, Julia," Trixie said, stepping onstage when Julia's song was over. "That was marvelous. And thank you, all of our Kiddie Kounselors who have performed this morning. I'm sorry to say that we are running a little late this morning and won't have time

74

to hear from Lila Fowler, so Lila will be first in tomorrow's lineup. I promise we'll schedule our time better for the rest of the week, so that nobody will be left out again!"

Jessica pretended not to notice the broad, triumphant grin on Lila's face.

"Oh, no!" Jessica wailed, staring in disbelief at Tuesday's activity roster.

"Is something wrong, Jessica?" Marcy asked.

Jessica forced herself to be pleasant. Marcy knew this place better than any of the counselors. She was one of the few people here who might turn out to be useful.

"No, not really," Jessica said. "I just wasn't expecting my little monsters to be finger painting with the other five- and six-year-olds this morning."

"Don't worry," Marcy said encouragingly. "It'll be messy—especially with your kids—but we use only water-based paints. They'll wash right off."

Jessica grimaced. She hadn't even considered the messes her happy little brats could make with finger paints. She'd been more concerned about the company she would be keeping while the munchkins were painting one another orange.

"What does it mean when the schedule says that all the five- and six-year-olds have painting at the Kiddie Kabana?" she asked, trying to sound as if it didn't matter very much. "Does that mean I'll be working with Lila and her kids this morning? I thought each counselor's group pretty much did things separately."

75

"Oh, no. Often, we put two groups together for certain activities," Marcy explained. "It's easier to clean up a dozen paint-spattered kids at once than it is to clean up six this morning and six this afternoon. Unfortunately for you, you're still responsible for your own kids, and Lila's responsible for hers. Obviously the two of you don't get along very well, though it's hard to understand why—you seem so much alike."

"We're definitely not alike," Jessica said ruefully.

But she smiled as another thought occurred to her. Two hours of finger painting with her six little brats should offer plenty of opportunity for revenge on the person who was responsible for her week of misery.

Lila was about to pay for her treachery.

"Yoo-hoo!" called Enid, stepping carefully up the fold-down ladder to the Wakefield attic Tuesday morning. "Wow, I didn't know your parents had installed a sauna up here!"

"That's certainly what it feels like," Elizabeth agreed.

Enid climbed off the ladder and onto the rough, plank floor. Elizabeth, covered with dust, was sitting on a trunk surrounded by cardboard boxes.

"You look like you've been here for hours," Enid said.

"Only since eight thirty or so. We've got specially formulated, fast-working dust up here. Stick around. You'll be as grimy as I am in no time!"

"That's us," Enid quipped. "Partners in grime!

What exactly are you looking for?"

"I wish I knew," Elizabeth said, shaking her head. "Anything that will prove Mom's innocence, I guess. I mean, I know it's not in her character to have an affair. We just have to find proof that will confirm it."

"This could be a wild-goose chase," Enid warned. "I mean," she added quickly, "I know your mother would never have an affair, but that's kind of a hard thing to prove, isn't it? It's not as though we're going to find character references and signed testimony saying she's a faithful wife."

Elizabeth sighed. "I know. But there's so much stuff up here—I'm sure we can find something that will prove it to Bruce. And in the meantime, we can be on the lookout for anything interesting to include in my English project."

A girl Jessica didn't recognize entered the Kiddie Kabana area, leading Lila's six well-behaved HLKs.

"Where's Lila?" Jessica asked the dark-haired girl, who looked about eighteen.

"One of the club employees took her on a tour of the island," the girl replied. "She hired me to watch her group until just before lunchtime."

Jessica was furious. "But it's against the rules. Lila's supposed to watch the kids herself!" she said.

"I'm saving up for college," the girl said with a shrug. "When someone offers me a lot of money for an easy job like this, I don't ask questions. I work at a formal wear shop at the adult club, but I can use all the extra money I can get. By the way, my name's Renata."

"I'm Jessica Wakefield," Jessica said numbly. "Which employee is taking Lila on a tour?"

"Mick Myers," Renata said dreamily. "Do you know him?"

"I've, uh, seen him around," Jessica said.

"He's gorgeous!" Renata said. "Your friend Lila is very lucky to be going out with him."

"She's not my friend," Jessica said pointedly. But her mind was racing. She had come up with the perfect way to pay Lila back. It was the only thing that could make her week of indentured slavery bearable.

Jessica was going to steal Mick Myers away from Lila.

Chapter 6

It was only eleven o'clock Tuesday morning, but Julia was starving. She didn't think she could wait until noon, when it would be time to take her seven- and eight-year-olds to lunch.

Until then, she was stuck here in the Kiddie Korral, watching a boring puppet show. She kept a strict eye on her six charges, who fidgeted in the row ahead of her. She chuckled quietly, thinking of the little brats that Jessica was stuck with. Jessica deserved them.

Charles was in the audience with his own group of seven- and eight-year-olds, sitting directly across the aisle from Julia. Two groups of older kids were also in the Kiddie Korral. One group was Marcy's. The other was led by either Howard or Harold, the anemic little counselors that Julia couldn't tell apart. They were too weird to waste time on, she had decided. Not like Charles. Charles had possibilities.

Julia turned to look thoughtfully at Charles. He certainly wasn't the best-looking guy around, but he was kind of cute, in a skinny, big-eared way. And he seemed sweet. More important, he was male. Julia was sick of being ignored by boys.

Julia sighed. Like most guys, Charles had no taste in girls. Why did boys always fall for girls like that obnoxious Jessica Wakefield? It just wasn't fair. Anyone could see that Jessica couldn't care less about Charles, but he hung on every word she said. Guys never looked at Julia in that worshipful kind of way.

Boys never take a second look at you unless you're beautiful and slinky, with thin thighs and big blue eyes, she lamented.

Or big brown eyes, Julia amended, thinking of Lila. Lila had left that morning with the most gorgeous boy Julia had ever laid eyes on—Mick Myers, the windsurfing instructor. Even Jessica had seemed impressed, not to mention green with jealousy. It served Jessica right. Julia would never forgive Jessica for that comment about Julia's being too fat to have boys notice her.

Julia narrowed her gray eyes. She wished she could think of a way to get back at Jessica, but nothing came to mind. After all, nobody could be expected to think at a dull puppet show like this. Julia stood up and slipped across the aisle to Charles.

"Charles," she whispered, kneeling in the aisle beside him. "I'm feeling ill. I think I'd better go back to my cabin to lie down. Would you mind keeping an eye on my kids until lunchtime?"

*   *   *

"Bobby," Jessica asked late Tuesday morning in the Kiddie Kabana, "who told you that you could finger paint all over the wall of the concession stand?"

"Lorenzo told me I could."

"I did not!" Lorenzo yelled. "He thought it up himself."

"He's lying!" screamed Bobby. "I did not think it up myself."

"I'm going to bite you!"

"Quiet, both of you!" Jessica yelled. She glanced over at Renata, who was watching with amusement from the other side of the Kabana. Of course, Renata was supposed to be taking care of Lila's Happy Little Kampers. But Lila's kids didn't seem to need much of her attention. The six darling children sat around two tables, cheerfully finger painting—on paper. Hardly a drop of paint marred their clean white smocks.

Jessica's group, on the other hand, looked like they'd been attacked by a mob of crazed house-painters. To make matters worse, they had managed to spatter pink paint in Jessica's hair.

She felt somebody tugging on the hem of her shorts. "Do you like my picture, Jessica?" Suzy asked. "It's a picture of you screaming at us."

"I like Bobby's picture best," Maria said. "He used lots of purple. I like purple."

Bobby turned to Maria with a grin. "I can make you purple, too," he offered.

Maria's blue eyes lit up. "Really?"

"No, he can't!" Jessica yelled. "You kids are not allowed to paint one another—or the walls! Is that clear?"

"I like a forceful woman," said the smoothest,

sexiest voice Jessica had ever heard.

She whirled to see blond, gorgeous Mick Myers, leaning against a tree that grew just outside the Kabana. He was even taller than she had thought, with a perfect body—muscular, but lean. His grin was incredibly sexy, his eyes were deep blue, and he had a cleft in his chin.

For a second, Jessica turned to look at the six children. Did she dare leave them on their own, even for a few minutes?

She smiled at Mick and tossed her hair over her shoulders to hide the pink paint spatters. Then she walked toward him, trying to look as sexy as she could in the baggy khaki shorts.

Julia walked along the quiet path to the Kiddie Kabana, chuckling to herself. It had been surprisingly easy to get Charles to watch her kids for her. Most guys would go out of their way only for a girl who looked like Jessica or Lila.

Then she sighed. Charles barely knew she was alive. He was just doing her a favor because he felt sorry for her.

Julia wasn't sure how she felt about Charles. But she was at Club Paradise—well, sort of—and she was determined to have a romance with *somebody* before the week was over. Charles wasn't Mick Myers, but at least he was in her league. She ought to have a chance with a boy like him.

"And I *would* have a chance with him," she whispered, "if it weren't for Jessica Wakefield leading him on!"

She rounded the last bend in the path and skidded to a halt. Just a few feet ahead, Jessica was talking with Mick. Behind them, her six bratty little HLKs scampered among the tables of Kiddie Kabana, smearing paint on everything in sight.

Julia quickly jumped behind a bush. From there, she could hear every word of Jessica's and Mick's conversation.

"I thought you were taking Lila on a tour this morning," Jessica said.

"We just got back," Mick acknowledged. "But don't worry about Lila. There's nothing between me and her. It's *you* that I've been noticing, Jessica."

Mick gazed at Jessica with his sexy blue eyes. Julia felt her own heart flutter.

"I've noticed you around, too," Jessica said, batting her long eyelashes.

What a disgusting flirt! Julia thought.

"I hear you're the windsurfing instructor," Jessica said. "It must be wonderful, out there on the water . . ."

Mick ran a hand through his long, blond hair. "It's awesome," he agreed. "Do you windsurf?"

"No, but I've always wanted to learn."

Jessica looked up at Mick expectantly, and Julia rolled her eyes. How much more obvious could Jessica get? She was blatantly hinting for a windsurfing date with Mick.

"I think that could be arranged," Mick said. He glanced at his expensive-looking wristwatch.

Waterproof, Julia decided, scrutinizing the watch. *It's probably worth a fortune.*

"What are you doing around two o'clock this afternoon?"

Jessica made a face and gestured at the pandemonium behind her. "Taking those screaming monsters on a nature walk."

"Can you find someone to cover for you?" Mick asked, resting a strong, tanned hand on Jessica's slim arm. "I'm sure I could make it worth your while."

Julia shook her head. Surely someone as perfect as Mick would realize about three minutes into their date that Jessica was a total airhead. But Jessica would still get to go out with him. Julia wished that just once, she could have an opportunity like that—a chance to prove to the Jessica Wakefields of the world that there was more to life than a perfect body with a perfect tan.

"You're on!" Jessica agreed. "I'll dupe *somebody* into taking this zoo off my hands." She ran back to the Kabana to pull apart Lorenzo and Karen, who were wrestling in green paint.

Mick turned on his heel just as Julia stepped out from behind the bush.

"Hi," Mick said absentmindedly.

Julia knew that her voice was her only asset, so she concentrated on putting into it every ounce of sexiness she could muster. "Hello," she said. "It's Mick, isn't it?"

"Windsurfing was great, Mick!" Jessica said at dinner Tuesday evening.

Things were definitely looking up. Her suitcase had arrived at lunchtime, in time for her to wear her

84

skimpy new bikini for windsurfing with Mick that afternoon. Now she was having an early dinner with him in an outdoor café overlooking the ocean. She was still wearing the black bathing suit, under a white, open-weave cover-up that she hoped Elizabeth wouldn't miss.

"You were a great student!" Mick said, slowly combing his fingers through his long, blond hair to arrange it perfectly behind his shoulders. "Of course, you did have the world's greatest teacher."

"I sure did," Jessica agreed, wanting to run her own fingers through his silky hair.

"How did you manage to get away from the little monsters this afternoon?"

"One of the other counselors—this guy named Charles—took them for me. Our kids were scheduled to go on a nature walk together, so I asked him if he could handle the whole lot." She smiled coyly. "Charles seemed happy to help."

"I can see why," Mick said, grasping her hand across the table. Jessica's heart fluttered as she looked into his piercing blue eyes. "Should I be jealous of this Charles character?"

"Absolutely not," Jessica said, making a face. "Charles is not at all my type."

"Am I your type?" Mick asked. He raised her hand to his lips and kissed it. Jessica thought she would melt at the touch of his soft, moist lips. "Do you go for tall, attractive guys with great bodies and long, sexy hair?"

"Oh, yes," Jessica said softly, smiling at him. Mick's self-assurance was almost intoxicating. Then she bit her lip and pouted in her sexiest way. "But what about Lila Fowler?" she asked. "You went out with her this morning. Should *I* be jealous?"

"That mousy brunette?" Mick asked. "Don't worry your pretty blond head about that spoiled rich kid," he said. "I really wanted to get out of it, but you know how it is—she's the boss's niece. I couldn't risk ticking off old Jimmo."

Jessica smiled. This was exactly what she had been wanting to hear. "So you're not really going out with her anymore?"

Mick shook his head ruefully. "I wish I didn't have to," he said, slowly running his fingers along Jessica's arm. "I'd rather save every spare moment for my golden goddess. But I have to take her to the disco tonight. You know how it is—in the line of duty and all that. I assumed you knew I had a date with Lila tonight. You two go to school together—you must talk."

Jessica shook her head. "Not anymore," she said resolutely. "We used to be friends, but Lila blew it. She lied to me, and brought me here under false pretenses. I'll never forgive her."

"So you two girls aren't speaking to each other at all?" Mick asked, with a thoughtful expression on his face.

"Absolutely not," Jessica said. "We haven't said a word to each other since the night we arrived, and I don't plan to say another word to her, ever again."

Mick nodded. "I can see why," he said. "Lila doesn't deserve a friend like you. I think you're right to stay away from her completely—at least for the rest of the week."

By the time Mick walked her to the front of her cabin that evening, Jessica thought she was in love.

"I want us to be together tomorrow evening, right about this time," Mick said, placing his hands on her shoulders. "I know a secluded little lagoon that's just perfect for watching the sun set over the ocean. It's always been my secret place. I've never brought anyone there before, but now I want you to see it, Jessica. I'll borrow a club Jeep if you can arrange to get away."

Jessica nodded. "I'll ask Charles to take my kids to dinner with his group."

"I'm sure he'll do it," Mick said. "You strike me as the kind of girl who can convince a boy to do whatever she wants."

"And do you know what I want right now?" Jessica asked breathlessly.

"Let's say I have a hunch," Mick murmured. He leaned forward, pulling her close to him. With his warm, soft lips, Mick gave Jessica the sexiest kiss she had ever received.

Now Jessica was *sure* she was in love.

The look Lila flashed her as Jessica entered the room almost made up for the terrible trick her ex-friend had played on her. Jessica smiled triumphantly and brushed by Lila, not minding the fact that she herself would be watching the six little monsters in another hour, while Lila danced with Mick at the club disco.

I'm the one Mick really likes, Jessica reminded herself smugly. And tomorrow night, Jessica would be the one running her fingers through Mick's gorgeous golden hair.

Revenge was definitely sweet.

Tuesday night, Lila ran her fingers through Mick Myers's gorgeous blond hair. She loved the feel of his strong arms around her as they danced to a slow, sensuous song with a Latin beat.

"You are the most beautiful girl on this island," Mick whispered into her ear. "Dancing together like this, we make the best-looking couple in the Caribbean."

Lila smiled. Mick wasn't nearly as wealthy as the boys she usually preferred to date, but he was definitely her kind of guy—the kind who could tell right off just how special she was. And she had never seen any boy who was better-looking.

Still, there was one issue that had to be cleared up. No boy, no matter how cute, would make a fool of Lila Fowler. She stopped dancing and took a step back, facing him squarely.

"What about Jessica Wakefield?" she asked pointedly.

Mick rolled his eyes. "That dumb blonde?" he asked. "I'm really sorry about that, Lila. But you know how pushy she is. And we regular staff members have been told to make nice with the temporary counselors. She kept bugging me to go out with her, and I didn't think I really had a choice."

Lila sighed, relieved. She knew better than anyone just how insistent Jessica could be when she wanted something. "Jessica has been acting like a spoiled child since Sunday night. After all, I've given her an all-expense-paid week in the Caribbean. Some people are never satisfied. She has no right to treat me as if I've committed some sort of crime!"

"It's hard to believe you two are the same age," Mick said. "You are so much more mature than Jessica is." He stroked her face with his finger. "And so unbelievably lovely."

Lila sighed and kissed him on the cheek.

"Lila, I've only known you for one day," Mick continued. "But you're the only girl I've ever felt this way about. You're the one I'm really interested in—certainly not Jessica. I know I'm not nearly good enough for a girl as classy and elegant as you are, but I'd like to spend every spare moment this week with my brown-eyed goddess."

Lila couldn't believe her ears. Mick was perfect— or, at least he would be if he had money, she admitted. But money didn't matter for a relationship that could only last a week. Other things were more important—the fact that he was drop-dead gorgeous, for instance. And the way he instinctively knew how to say exactly the right thing.

I must really like him, Lila thought with a laugh, *or I would never think that money doesn't matter!* But she didn't care. She was going to have a wonderful, romantic week with Mick. And Jessica would just have to live with that. Lila couldn't wait to see Jessica's face when she told her what Mick had said about her—"dumb blonde," "pushy," and "immature"! Mick was certainly a good judge of character, Lila thought. Jessica would be absolutely livid when she heard about it.

But I can't tell Jessica, Lila thought ruefully, *because we're not speaking.*

"Let me prove to you that you're the only girl I care about," Mick whispered into her ear, making her forget all about Jessica. "There's this secluded little lagoon I know. It's always been my secret place, and I've never brought anyone there. But now I want *you* to see it. I can borrow a club Jeep tomorrow afternoon and we can go for a private swim. Can you get away?"

"It sounds fabulous," Lila said. "And I'm sure I can get Renata to take my kids for a few hours after lunch."

"That doesn't surprise me a bit," Mick said. "You strike me as the kind of girl who can convince anyone to do just about anything she wants."

"Speaking of convincing," Lila said, "do you know any of the guys in the band personally? I'm responsible for arranging some entertainment for the kids tomorrow morning. I thought some of the band members might help."

"Between your looks and your uncle," Mick said, "I'm sure they'll do whatever you ask."

Lila narrowed her eyes with determination. "Good," she said, "because I plan to put on the best welcome show in Kiddie Paradise history!"

The pretty blond woman pushed open the door and strode into the room, looking determined but nervous.

Inside the room, a middle-aged man disentangled himself from an embrace with a tall woman in a black negligee. The blond woman advanced on the couple with a hurt look in her eyes. She thrust a gun forward

*in her trembling hands. Her husband backed into a
corner as his girlfriend scurried for cover.*

*The blond woman fired the gun—once, twice . . .
five times—and the man fell to the floor. She turned
the gun on the woman in the black negligee. . . .*

Elizabeth turned on the light. This was ridiculous.
It was Tuesday night and she couldn't get *Adam's Rib*
out of her mind. It was only a movie! Why couldn't
she forget about it and get some sleep?

Elizabeth felt sick. What if it happened in real
life? What if Mrs. Patman followed Mr. Patman and
Alice Wakefield to Chicago and shot him—or shot
both of them?

Katharine Hepburn had played the lawyer who
defended the woman in her trial for attempted mur-
der. Hepburn had argued that society could accept a
man who committed violence to defend his honor.
She said a woman was held to a different standard.

That double standard was certainly true of Bruce,
Elizabeth thought. He considered Alice Wakefield to
be the home-wrecker who had come between his
parents. But wasn't his father just as much of a home-
wrecker, coming between Mr. and Mrs. Wakefield?

And what if it was Bruce behind that gun, aiming
at Alice Wakefield?

Hold on, Elizabeth cautioned herself. *You're getting carried away! You don't even believe they're having an affair, right?*

She lay back against her pillow, miserable. She
missed Todd terribly, and she wished Jessica were
home to talk to.

"I guess it's just as well that she's away," Elizabeth

said out loud. "At least one of us is having a good vacation."

"Top that, Jessica Wakefield!" Lila said under her breath as the last chord of "I Just Want to Say Hello" resonated through the Kiddie Korral early Wednesday morning. It was the hit single from rock star Jamie Peters' new CD, and the ensemble from the club disco had played it well, if the audience's enthusiastic applause was any indication.

Of course, Lila had been playing too—softly, on a borrowed marimba. But she had only joined in because it was supposed to be *her* welcome act in Wednesday morning's presentations, and she was required to participate. She was pretty good on the marimba, she thought, but she wasn't about to humiliate herself by soloing on an instrument few people had the sense to appreciate.

"Thank you, Lila, for arranging such a fun treat for all of us this morning," Trixie said, quieting the applause. "I don't think I've ever had a counselor work so hard to come up with something special for our morning welcome show."

Lila glared triumphantly at Jessica, who sat toward the back of the open-air auditorium, looking dejected. Unfortunately for Jessica, she didn't have Lila's money or connections—not to mention her talent. Lila knew that cheerleading and flirting were the only things Jessica had ever been good at.

Lila smiled wickedly. She couldn't wait to see how her former best friend was going to make a fool of herself today.

Jessica's heart sank. Lila, that rat, had avoided being embarrassed in front of everybody. Jessica was sure Lila had used her connection with her uncle to get some real musicians for her Wednesday-morning welcome act. Meanwhile, Jessica was going to have to perform another humiliating routine, all by herself. Her cheerleading act the day before had bombed. The only other thing Jessica had been able to come up with was a modern dance number.

"I'm a good dancer!" she reminded herself under her breath. But she was afraid that her act would look amateurish after Lila's. She just hoped Trixie the Pixie wouldn't call on her to go next.

"Next," Trixie announced, "we'll hear from Jessica Wakefield!"

As Jessica slipped her background music into the tape deck Trixie had provided, she noticed her own group of six children tiptoeing up the aisle.

"Uh-oh," Jessica said aloud. There was no telling what the Happy Little Monsters were planning. Jessica thought the expressions on their faces seemed a little too happy as they settled on the steps along the left side of the stage.

Still, she couldn't very well call off her act just because her own charges wanted to watch it. And for now, they did appear to be behaving themselves, though the way they were crouched on the steps reminded her of a pack of vultures, ready to spring.

Jessica had choreographed a simple, lighthearted dance routine. She started with a few easy kicks and began to relax. *Maybe this won't be so bad,* she thought. At least the audience didn't look bored. Some of the counselors were even smiling. Charles was positively beaming.

As Jessica launched into her first cartwheel, she caught sight of a suspicious movement among her Happy Little Vultures. Gerry Pat stood up and was slowly inching his way around the front of the stage.

What is he up to? she thought frantically.

As she neared her act's finale, Jessica felt sick with dread. She knew the little brats were planning something to humiliate her. Lorenzo, Bobby, and Karen were grinning like Cheshire cats. Maria and Suzy had their heads together and seemed to be giggling. Even worse, Gerry Pat had reached the opposite side of the stage. He was kneeling alone on the top step, with a serious expression on his freckled face.

Jessica was supposed to end her dance with a difficult leap, landing on one leg. Her takeoff was good. But then she saw something rolling beneath her.

Jessica would never forget the feel of Gerry Pat's hard, round marble beneath her sneaker. She rolled forward and skidded a few feet. Then, with a loud, hollow-sounding thump, she landed gracelessly on the hard, wooden stage.

The audience was silent for a long, terrible moment. Then Jessica heard snickering. She wished the stage would collapse and swallow her up. When it became clear that Jessica wasn't injured, the snickers from the audience turned into full-blown laughter. Even Trixie couldn't suppress a giggle. And Jessica could hear Lila laughing louder than anyone.

Lorenzo darted forward and snatched several tiny

objects from the stage. Nobody else seemed to have noticed him.

"Your attention, please!" Trixie pleaded into the microphone as Charles helped Jessica to the nearest bench. The laughter quieted. "Thank you, Jessica," Trixie continued cheerfully. "You certainly get an E for effort!"

"And a K for klutziness!" called Julia.

Jessica glared at her Happy Little Monsters, who looked happier than they'd looked all week. Obviously, they'd all been in on this together. Lorenzo met her stare with a smug set to his mouth and a challenge in his beady eyes. Gerry Pat glanced at Lorenzo for approval and then thumbed his nose at her. Karen stuck out her tongue.

I will *get control of them,* she vowed. *I have to.*

Chapter 7

"Karen, you stay here by the pool with Suzy," Jessica said late Wednesday morning. "And don't either of you go in the water until I get back with the other kids."

Karen shook her head. "My mommy says I'm supposed to watch Suzy, so she can go in the water if I say so!"

"No, she can't!" Jessica yelled at the skinny six-year-old. "I have to go find the others, wherever they ran off to. I can't believe they could disappear so quickly. Until I get back, you'll both stay near the pool, but out of the water and out of trouble. Do you understand me?"

In response, Karen stuck out her long tongue until its tip touched her nose. Suzy tried, unsuccessfully, to mimic her.

Jessica looked around again for Charles. Certainly he would watch the two girls for a few minutes, if she flattered him a little bit. But Charles and his group were nowhere to be seen. She remembered that they were playing on the beach this morning, not by the pool. The only counselor nearby was Lila, and she was the last person Jessica would ask for help.

"I know something you don't know!" Suzy said suddenly, in a singsong voice. "I know where Maria and the boys are."

"Why the heck didn't you say so?" Jessica almost screamed. "Where are they?"

The little girl put her hands behind her back and swayed from side to side. "It's a secret. And you're mean, so I'm not going to tell."

Jessica knelt down and grabbed Suzy by the shoulders. "Suzy, tell me right now where the other kids have disappeared to. If I have to go look for them, it'll be a long time before you can go in the pool."

"No, it won't," Suzy said reasonably. "We'll go in the pool as soon as you go away."

"Fine!" Jessica said, exasperated. "Go in the pool! But don't complain to me if Larry the Lifeguard yells at you. I'm going to find the other kids."

Jessica saw the boys and Maria as she came around the corner of the boys' cabin. They were still wearing their bathing suits; a purple towel covered Maria's hair.

"Where have you little jerks been all this time?" Jessica demanded. "You're supposed to be at the pool with the rest of us. What made you decide to wander off—"

Jessica stopped and looked from child to child.

"Why are you grinning?" she asked, not sure she wanted to hear the answer. "Bobby, what are you hiding behind your back?"

"Nothing," Bobby said, holding out his hands for inspection. They were empty and deep purple.

"Do you want to see some magic tricks?" he asked innocently.

"No, I don't want to see some magic tricks! We're going back to the pool right now!"

"But Jessica—" Maria began.

"No arguments!"

She grabbed Maria's hand and began to pull her along. The towel fell off Maria's head and fell to the sand. Jessica gasped.

Maria's curly hair was bright purple.

Jessica leaned weakly against the side of the bunkhouse. "Is somebody going to tell me why Maria's hair is purple?"

"Isn't it always that color?" asked Gerry Pat.

"I didn't have anything to do with it," said Lorenzo. "And I'll bite anyone who says I did!"

Jessica noticed purple stains on Maria's ears and forehead. Bobby was the only boy with hands the same shade.

"Bobby, why did you dye Maria's hair purple?"

"It was a trick," Bobby said, as though that explained everything.

"It's a nice color!" Maria said, pulling a long curl in front of her face to inspect the shade. "I like it."

"It's only finger paint," Bobby said. "I saved some of the paint we used yesterday. It'll come out with water."

"Good," Jessica said. "We'll go wash it out right now. And if any of you ever—"

She stopped, confused. Lorenzo was smiling much too broadly, and Gerry Pat began to giggle hysterically.

"Is there something else I should know about?" Jessica asked, looking from one boy to the other.

"Gerry Pat switched the paints," Lorenzo said. "He took the finger paints out of Bobby's jar and put some of the big kids' powdered dye in it instead. Her hair's going to be purple *forever*!"

Maria smiled up at Jessica. "My mommy's going to be very mad at you," she said sweetly. "She might yell."

Jessica had a brief but pleasant mental image of Lila with long, silky, purple hair. She fought the impulse to ask Gerry Pat if he had any extra dye.

Calm down, Jessica told herself. *I'm the counselor here. I have to stay calm and get control of the situation.*

First, of course, she had to get control of herself. She thought about Mick's long, sun-streaked hair and perfect eyes, and found herself relaxing a little. She only had to get through this rotten day, and then she would be watching the sunset with Mick in the secluded lagoon where he'd never taken any other girl—not even Lila. Jessica sighed, wishing she were there now.

Maria turned to the boys. "Can you make my eyes purple, too?" she asked.

On Wednesday morning, Elizabeth pulled her mother's old trunk directly under the attic's one light bulb. The trunk was the only thing left in the attic that she hadn't opened—it was her last chance. She began fiddling with the latch.

"Hello!" a voice called from the hallway below. "Are you up there, Liz? Your dad let me in on his way out. Can I come up?"

It was Amy.

"Sure, Amy," Elizabeth said as nicely as she could. She was annoyed. The contents of the trunk seemed like her last chance to clear her mother's name. But she couldn't open the trunk with Amy there. Elizabeth didn't want anyone else to hear about Bruce's accusations. And Amy was second only to Caroline Pearce when it came to spreading rumors in Sweet Valley. Elizabeth pushed the trunk aside and quickly opened one of the boxes she'd looked through the day before.

"Gee, it's dusty up here!" Amy said. "I hope you don't mind that I just popped on over without calling. But I had some free time this morning, and I figured you'd be working on your paper, too. Can you help me?"

"Not for too long, Amy," Elizabeth warned her. "I need the time for my own research. But I'll see what I can do. Tell me what you've got so far. Did you say you were writing about your great-great-grandmother? What do you know about her?"

Amy blushed and leafed through the notebook she had brought with her. Elizabeth could see that most of its pages were blank.

"I guess you couldn't find much," Elizabeth said.

Amy shook her head. "No. To tell you the truth, I don't know where to start."

"Is this great-great-grandmother on your mother's side of the family? Maybe you should start by interviewing your mother about everything she knows about her."

"I did," Amy said quickly. "I mean, I will. I was planning to interview her as soon as she has the time to sit down with me. But she's been awfully busy. What if it was your great-great-grandmother, Liz? Where is the first place you'd look?"

"If I were writing about my great-great-grandmother Jessamyn, I would start by interviewing any relatives who might have heard stories about her," Elizabeth said. "Including my father. Maybe my mother told him something interesting about Jessamyn."

Amy looked thoughtful. "That's not a bad idea," she said. "I wonder how I could manage that."

"I'm sure your father would be happy to help you," Elizabeth said. "Amy, I hate to kick you out, but I've got this trunk to go through this morning, before Enid comes to pick me up."

Amy suddenly seemed eager to leave. "Don't say another word! I'm keeping you from your own research. Thanks a bunch, Liz! I can see myself out."

Lila leaned back in her lounge chair by the pool late Wednesday morning, squinting into the sun.

"Bartholomew," she said sweetly, motioning to a small, fair-skinned boy with a crew cut. "I think I left my sunglasses back at the Korral this morning, on a chair near the aisle. Would you be a dear little boy and go find them for me?"

Bartholomew blushed and grinned, showing a gap where his front teeth should have been. Then he scurried away toward the Kiddie Korral.

"He got to help you last time!" Heidi complained. "Isn't it my turn yet?"

"It certainly is," Lila told the pretty six-year-old. "I was saving a very special job just for you, Heidi. Would you go up to the drink counter and get me an iced tea, sweetheart?"

Lila sighed as the dark-haired girl scampered away. Being assigned to the pool this morning was a stroke of luck. She could work on her tan, just in time for her date to swim with Mick in his private lagoon after lunch. Luckily, a few sexy smiles toward Larry had been enough to get the good-looking, dark-haired lifeguard to agree to watch her kids when they went in the water.

Lila didn't know what Jessica had been so worked up about all week. Baby-sitting wasn't so awful. Like anything else, it just took some talent.

"Some people have it," Lila said aloud, "and some people don't."

"Hi, Princess!" said a sexy voice. Lila opened her eyes and smiled. Mick was sitting on the edge of her lounge chair.

"Mick," she said, tilting her head so that her long, straight hair hung down at just the right angle, framing her sunlit face. "I wasn't expecting to see you this morning."

"I know," he said. "But I couldn't wait until our date this afternoon. I couldn't stop thinking about you after last night. Did I tell you what a terrific dancer you are?"

Lila laughed. "At least nine times."

"Make it an even ten," Mick said. "And did I tell you that you're the most beautiful girl I've ever seen? In fact, you look especially awesome in that bathing suit."

"You don't look so bad yourself," Lila said. Mick was wearing Club Paradise swim trunks and a loose, cutoff shirt that showed off his flat stomach and well-formed biceps. She laid a hand, lightly, on his tanned arm and felt a current, like electricity, running through her.

Mick smiled his sexiest smile and made a show of smoothing his hair—*as if every strand of Mick's perfect hair wasn't already in exactly the right place*, Lila thought admiringly.

Mick's blue eyes were almost hypnotic. For a moment, Lila felt apprehensive. This guy was just too attractive, if that was possible. It would be easy to fall for him completely. And Lila prided herself on always being in control of every situation.

But I am in control, she assured herself. Certainly, there could be no harm in just having a good time with Mick this week. And knowing that Jessica was infatuated with him made Mick even more intriguing—especially when he made it clear that he found Lila more attractive than Jessica.

Mick looked around at the pool area. Two of Jessica's little girls were chasing each other around as Larry the Lifeguard yelled at them. "Looks like Jessica's got her hands full," he said. "You know, I checked out this whole pool area from behind a tree before I showed myself. I didn't want to risk running into her— she might pester me to go out with her again!"

"If she only ran off to track down some of her rotten little brats, she could be back at any time."

"What about all the other Happy Little Koun-selors?" Mick asked. "I don't see that fat blob, Julia, anywhere. And where's Marcy, Mother Hen to the world? It looks like the whole staff has taken advantage of your generous nature, Lila. Have they all left you here alone to take care of everything?"

Lila sighed. It was a rare guy who appreciated how truly generous she was at heart. Most people didn't understand that someone with Lila's assets had to guard her generosity carefully, to keep the wrong people from trying to take advantage of her.

"Only Jessica and I have our groups at the pool this morning," Lila explained. "Though it does look like I'm stuck with her brats."

Of course, Lila hadn't taken the least bit of re-sponsibility for Jessica's kids—nothing could make her do that, after the way Jessica was snubbing her. But she couldn't pass up a chance to make herself look even better to Mick, while making Jessica seem irresponsible.

"I wish I could help you," Mick said in an under-standing voice. "But I have to give a windsurfing les-son to a couple of tourists at eleven-thirty. So I'd better go. But I won't leave until you promise to go out with me tomorrow night, as well as this after-noon. How about a moonlight swim off the pier near the yacht club?"

"That sounds heavenly."

"Speaking of heavenly," Mick said, grinning. "I was envisioning a particularly romantic evening. You should wear your very sexiest bathing suit."

Lila raised her eyebrows. "I will if you will, Mick."

After Mick was gone, Lila lay back in her lounge chair and closed her eyes, savoring the thought of their upcoming afternoon together.

A few minutes later, a commotion at the other end of the pool made Lila sit up and remove her sunglasses. Jessica was walking purposefully into the pool area, with four small children trailing after her. The three boys had evil grins on their faces. The little girl had bright purple hair.

Lila laughed. How did Jessica get herself into these situations?

"How do I get myself into these situations?" Jessica asked, scrubbing Maria's hair with a towel in the bathhouse by the pool.

"Am I still purple?" Maria asked cheerfully.

"Yes," Jessica said. "I was hoping I could at least tone it down to a dull lavender. But I can't get out a single drop of the purple. I'll have to check with Marcy and figure out what kind of dye this is. There must be some way to remove it."

"What's all that noise out there?" Maria asked.

"It has gotten a lot louder, hasn't it?" Jessica asked, with a sinking feeling. Lorenzo, Gerry Pat, and Bobby were out there with nobody to watch them. "Maybe if we stay here, it'll stop."

"I don't think so," Maria said, shaking her purple curls.

"Neither do I."

When Jessica and Maria emerged from the bathhouse, Jessica wanted to turn around and run right back in. Lorenzo, Gerry Pat, and Bobby had removed the rope that separated the shallow end of the pool from the deeper end, and had used it to tie four pretty little girls together. Now they were dancing around them, pelting the girls with water balloons.

The girls were crying, the boys were whooping, and Larry the Lifeguard was screaming at all of them.

Jessica's only consolation was that the little girls were part of Lila's group. Lila herself was sitting up in her lounge chair, keeping a wary eye on the water balloons. Her sunglasses were pushed on top of her head and she was halfheartedly trying to reason with Jessica's boys, who ignored her completely.

"Lila's such a fake," Jessica said to Maria, for lack of any other audience. "She couldn't care less about those little girls being tied up. She's only trying to stop the boys because they disturbed her sunbathing!"

Maria looked at her quizzically from under her mop of purple curls. "I still want my eyes dyed purple," she said.

"Get over here right now, Jessica!" Larry called, catching sight of her.

Jessica sighed miserably. The first time she'd seen the tall, dark-haired lifeguard, she'd considered flirting with him. But since the first time she'd brought her Happy Little Monsters to the pool, he'd treated her as if children were contagious. Baby-sitting was definitely putting a crimp in her social life.

Suddenly, Jessica couldn't take another minute of being inconvenienced and humiliated by the children's behavior. And she refused to be shown up in front of Lila again. It was time to show the little brats—and Lila—just who was in charge.

Jessica marched toward the commotion, more angry than she had ever been. Ignoring the threat of water balloons, she walked right up to the boys, grabbed Lorenzo's shoulder, and whirled him around.

"That's it, Lorenzo!" she yelled as loudly as she could. "You're going to untie that rope and let those girls go. And you're going to do it now!

"It's not my fault!" Lorenzo screamed. He pointed at Gerry Pat and Bobby. "They did it, too!"

"But you're the ringleader," Jessica said. "And you're going to be the one who stops this."

"You can't boss me," Lorenzo said smugly. "I'm my own boss." He weighed a loaded balloon in his hands, staring back and forth between it and Jessica's face.

"And you can't scare me," Jessica replied. "I'm already drenched from trying to wash that purple stuff out of Maria's hair. My clothes are a mess. My hair is a mess. I'm not afraid of a little water balloon. I've got nothing to lose!"

Lorenzo changed tactics. "I'll bite you!" he threatened.

"And I'll bite you right back."

Lorenzo's mouth dropped open. "You can't do that!" he said. "You're almost a grown-up, and grown-ups don't bite people!"

"This one does," Jessica warned.

She used her most threatening tone, but inside, she was shaking. Lorenzo had to obey her—just this once. After everything else that had happened today, she couldn't bear to have Lila see her defeated by a

107

six-year-old. She hoped Lorenzo was really a coward under all that bravado. Maybe nobody had ever called his bluff before.

"Those girls are no fun anyway," Lorenzo complained. "They're wimps. All they do is cry."

"*Our* girls are better than you fraidy-cat girls," Bobby said to Lila's four whimpering girls, as he began trying to untie the clumsy knots in the thick rope. "One of our girls can touch her nose with her tongue. I bet none of you can do that!"

"Karen!" Jessica said, whirling around. "Where are Karen and Suzy? Lorenzo, Bobby, Gerry Pat, and Maria!" Jessica called in the most commanding voice she could muster. "I want you to sit on those four chairs, right there. And stay there until I find the other two. If you move away from those chairs, Larry the Lifeguard is going to take that big, thick rope and tie you up with it. Is that clear?"

Jessica wasn't sure how long her authority would last, but she had made Lorenzo back down, and they all seemed a little scared of her. They just had to stay scared until the end of the afternoon, she told herself. Then she would go on her date with Mick, and everything would be all right.

Jessica sighed. Mick was busy all afternoon in a meeting of the water-sports instructors. When it was over, he would drive her to his secluded lagoon so they could spend a romantic evening together, watching the sky and sea and each other.

But first, Jessica had to find Karen and Suzy. It wasn't going to be easy surviving the afternoon.

*   *   *

Elizabeth coughed as she lifted the lid of her mother's old trunk in the attic late Wednesday morning. This was the hottest day yet. The temperature was over a hundred degrees. In the attic, she realized, it was probably even hotter than that.

The dusty old trunk was Elizabeth's last hope—not only for finding something really interesting to put into her family biography, but also to clear her mother's name. There had to be something in it that would prove beyond any doubt that Alice Wakefield couldn't possibly be having an affair with Henry Patman. There had to be. As soon as she found whatever it was, she would run downstairs and call Bruce to set up a meeting after that day's matinee of *Philadelphia Story.*

Elizabeth pulled out a layer of tissue paper that covered the rest of the trunk's contents, and then stopped, surprised. The trunk seemed to be filled with something filmy and white. She lifted a fold of the fabric, and realized that she had found a bridal veil. *This must be Mom's wedding trunk,* she realized with a thrill.

She carefully picked up the soft white veil and the elaborate headpiece it was attached to. Of course, Elizabeth had seen pictures of her parents' wedding, but she'd never noticed how beautiful her mother's headpiece was. Somehow, Elizabeth had remembered it as a simple wreath of flowers. She gently ran a finger over the pearls and tiny silk roses sewn along its edges.

She gingerly raised it to her head and slipped it over her hair, imagining herself processing slowly down a long aisle on her father's arm, as Todd waited up ahead. . . .

Elizabeth laughed nervously at herself and set the veil aside. This was no time for daydreaming. She had a mission to complete. She cleared away another layer of tissue paper from the trunk. White satin gleamed like moonlight in the dim attic. This was her mother's wedding gown, she realized as she carefully unfolded it from the trunk.

Elizabeth stood up and held the dress in front of her. It wasn't at all the kind of dress she would imagine her simple, straightforward mother choosing. It looked so much more elaborate than it did in the photographs she had seen. But Elizabeth had taken enough pictures to know you couldn't always capture the details with a camera.

Now, she ran her hands over the hundreds of tiny pearls that studded the bodice, fingered the yellowing lace around the neckline, and felt the hot, heavy satin rustle against her legs.

She laid the gown across a row of boxes and knelt down again beside the trunk. She pulled out a pair of white satin pumps with impossibly high, pencil-thin heels. A huge, dried bouquet of white cabbage roses looked too delicate to touch, so Elizabeth left it in the trunk. But under it was something else—something wrapped in tissue paper. A framed photograph.

Elizabeth unwound the tissue paper, wiped the dust off the glass, and looked down at her mother, who was smiling softly in the elegant satin dress.

And standing beside her, wearing a black tuxedo, was Henry Patman!

Chapter 8

Julia frowned at her reflection in the full-length mirror of the counselors' cabin. In less than half an hour, she would be meeting Mick for lunch—for the second day in a row! This time, she wanted to look perfect for him.

Yesterday's lunch date with Mick had come up so suddenly that Julia didn't have time to change her clothes. He had asked her out when they met in the woods near the Kiddie Kabana, after she eavesdropped on his conversation with Jessica. Despite her baggy denim shorts and wrinkled camp shirt, Tuesday's lunch date had been wonderful. Mick even seemed to think she was pretty. He said he liked his women "voluptuous." He said that Jessica and Lila were both too thin, and that he didn't plan to date either of them again.

Julia had been right about Mick. He was perfect.

Julia appraised herself as she tucked her tank top

into her pleated jeans. "I'm not fat," she said, trying to believe it. "I'm voluptuous."

The tank top was barer than she usually liked to wear, but it made her look really curvy on top, she decided. If Mick was focusing on her daring neckline, maybe he wouldn't notice the size of her hips and the whiteness of her upper arms.

The door opened behind her and Julia jumped, embarrassed to be caught staring at herself in the mirror.

"Oh. Hi, Lila," she said quickly.

"Hello, Julia," Lila replied coolly as she sauntered into the cabin. "I didn't notice you there."

As usual, Lila looked elegant, regal, and in control—as though she owned the place, Julia thought. Of course, Lila practically did own the place. Or her uncle did, which was almost as good.

Of the two Southern Californians, Julia definitely preferred Lila to Jessica. And Lila might be a useful ally. Julia still wanted to make Jessica pay for saying Julia was too fat to attract boys; Lila had known Jessica for a long time and might be able to help Julia get back at her.

Of course, Lila would also be disappointed when everyone heard which girl Mick really liked. So Julia decided to keep her relationship with Mick a secret for now. She would wait for the perfect time to spring the news on Jessica—preferably a time when Jessica would be embarrassed in front of a lot of people. Julia grinned, imagining the look on Jessica's face when she found out that Mick liked Julia best.

Then she turned back to the mirror and tried to fluff out her bangs.

"Lila, how do you make your hair look so perfect in this heat?"

Lila swept her silky brown hair over her shoulder. "I suppose I was just born with perfect hair."

On second thought, maybe Lila isn't much better than Jessica, Julia decided. *She's certainly just as conceited.*

Julia was torn between dislike, envy, and pragmatism. Pragmatism won. Lila could be more useful as a friend than an enemy. She smiled. "You were just born perfect, period."

"That's true," Lila agreed. "But I don't know why the heat should affect your hair. It isn't that hot here."

No, not if you're an ice princess, Julia thought.

"You probably know about the terrible heat wave we've been having at home in California," Lila continued. "I'm sure it's worse than anything you could imagine."

"Well, I'm from Wisconsin," Julia said. "And believe me, this is hot!"

"Wisconsin?" Lila asked, managing to sound polite and derisive at the same time.

Julia didn't like the implication that there was something wrong with coming from Wisconsin, but she was impressed with the way Lila had conveyed her scorn in such a civilized manner. *I could learn a lot from her,* she thought.

Julia checked her watch to make sure she wasn't going to be late meeting Mick at the entrance to

113

Kiddie Paradise. "It's not lunchtime yet," she said. "How did you get out of looking after your kids this morning?"

"Where there's a bill, there's a way," Lila explained with a bored expression. "Especially when it's a ten or a twenty. It's not hard to find a baby-sitter, if you have the right resources. I have plans for this afternoon, and I wanted to use lunchtime to get ready."

"Well, I have plans, too," Julia said. "I've got to meet, uh, someone. I'll see you later, Lila!"

Elizabeth stared at the photograph. The dimness of the attic, combined with her confusion about Bruce's accusations, had to be playing tricks on her eyes.

This can't be a picture of my mother marrying Bruce's father. That's impossible.

She stood up and held the faded photograph near the unshaded light bulb that hung overhead. Sure enough, the photo showed the twins' mother in her early twenties, looking a lot like Elizabeth. She was wearing the elaborate white gown and veil that Elizabeth had pulled out of the trunk just a few minutes earlier. And beside her stood a young Henry Patman, dressed in an expensive tuxedo and looking surprisingly like Bruce.

For a moment, Elizabeth wanted to laugh hysterically. The photograph reminded her of a middle-school experiment in which Elizabeth and Bruce had pretended to be married to each other.

But this was no game.

There was no doubt about it. Before she became

114

Alice Wakefield, Elizabeth's mother had been married to Henry Patman.

Elizabeth felt as if she were suffocating. Everything she knew about her mother—and her whole family—was wrong. Suddenly, Bruce's wild stories seemed a lot less wild.

Mick helped Lila out of the little red Club Paradise Jeep.

"Welcome to my private paradise," he said, wrapping a muscular arm around her shoulders. He swept back her hair and kissed her. Lila felt her entire body tingle.

"How do you like it so far?" he asked.

"Very impressive." Lila gestured at the swaying palm trees and the quiet, turquoise water of the lagoon. A crescent of sandy beach gleamed white in the afternoon sun, with a few large boulders sheltering it on one end. "Your decorator did a marvelous job. And the customer service is excellent."

"We aim to please, madam," Mick said, strolling with her to the water's edge. He took Lila in his arms and gave her a long, sensuous kiss.

"It was agony, Lila," he said a few minutes later, "sitting through that long, boring lunch meeting with the other water-sports instructors, thinking of you and counting the minutes until we could be together again."

Lila stared at him. "Meeting? But you said you had to give a windsurfing lesson to some tourists."

"I did?" Mick asked. "Well, yes. First, I gave the windsurfing lesson, and then I spent the rest of the afternoon in the meeting. We had to go over some new safety policies for water sports. It was pretty important stuff, but not nearly as mesmerizing as looking into your beautiful brown eyes, Lila."

He kissed her again, and Lila felt herself melting like chocolate in his arms.

Lila pulled away and smiled. "This place is wonderful," she told Mick.

"So is the company. Along with being the prettiest girl on this island, Lila, you are really special."

"I wish I could just stay here all week and leave the little Kampers to fend for themselves."

"Speaking of the brats, how did you manage to get away from them for the afternoon?"

"Oh, it wasn't hard to find someone to fill in for me," Lila said with a shrug. "I've got those little kids behaving so well that they're a baby-sitter's dream."

"You have a way with people of all ages," Mick said. Then he laughed. "But I don't know about this Bartholomew character you told me about. It sounds like he's got a big-time crush on you."

"I don't think you have anything to worry about," Lila said. "I like my men a little more mature than that. He's only five."

"Good. Because I know someone else who's got a big-time crush on you, too. And he doesn't like to share."

"And who would that be?"

"A certain extremely handsome windsurfer with great hair, terrific biceps, and eyes only for you."

Lila sighed and leaned back against him. She was the luckiest girl on this island—she was beautiful, rich, and talented. And she had Mick. She couldn't help thinking about the other counselors, back at Kiddie Paradise.

She remembered the way that Julia had eyed her with such wistfulness in their cabin before lunch. *In her wildest dreams,* Lila thought, *Julia could never date anyone like Mick.*

Then there was Jessica. *Sure, Jessica is attractive enough,* Lila supposed, *if you like loud, unsubtle blondes.*

Luckily, Mick had more sense than that.

"Lila," he whispered into her ear. "You may think this is crazy, since I've known you for only two days. But I think I'm falling in love."

Lila whirled around, surprised and pleased. She didn't think she was exactly *in love* with Mick. But she liked him more than she had liked any boy in a long time. And she always felt that the healthiest kind of relationship was with a guy who needed her just a little bit more than she needed him.

"It's like a steam bath out there," Elizabeth said on Wednesday afternoon as she leaned back into the comfortable leather seat of Bruce's air-conditioned Porsche.

Outside, the temperature was a hundred and five degrees. Even the ocean looked hot. Low waves rolled listlessly into shore, lapping against the sand as if they had expended all their energy far out at sea.

"So, what did you want to talk to me about?" Bruce demanded.

Elizabeth opened her mouth, but closed it again.

How can I possibly tell him? she wondered, staring out the window.

"Come on, Wakefield," Bruce urged. "I don't have all day. You said you had something important to tell me. I'm surprised you didn't bring your two sidekicks along, too. Wouldn't that be cozy?"

"I haven't told Enid and Olivia anything about this," said Elizabeth. "I wanted to talk to you first. I just asked Enid to drop me off here after *Philadelphia Story.* I told her I wanted to walk along the beach for a while."

"I guess it runs in the family," Bruce said bitterly. "I mean, planning secret rendezvous with men. Like mother, like daughter."

"Stop it, Bruce!" Elizabeth said sharply. "This is important! I was looking through an old trunk of my mom's this morning, trying to find something that would prove to you once and for all that my mother never loved any man but my father. Here's what I found instead."

She handed Bruce the photograph and watched his eyes widen with surprise and hurt. For once, she could sympathize completely with Bruce Patman.

"Married?" he whispered, sounding as if he'd been punched in the stomach. "They were married to each other, and they never told us?"

"I can't think of any other explanation," Elizabeth admitted.

Then an unspeakable thought occurred to Elizabeth, and she stared at Bruce, terrified.

"Could that mean that we—" he began in a horrified voice, and Elizabeth knew he was thinking the same thing.

Quickly, she subtracted the years in her head.

"No," she said, with a sigh of relief. "We couldn't be brother and sister. My parents had been married for several years before Jessica and I were born."

"You're right," Bruce decided. Elizabeth had never seen him look so pale.

"Oh, my gosh!" she said suddenly. "What about my brother Steven? Could he be your—"

"No, he couldn't be my brother. Steven's two years older than you, and a year older than me. Your parents had already been married a couple years when he was born, right?"

"Yes, of course. You're right. Besides, Steven looks so much like my father that I don't know how I could imagine he wasn't his son."

"That's not all I'm right about," Bruce said. "This proves that I've been right all along. Your mother and my father are having an affair."

Chapter 9

Jessica dipped her toes in the warm Caribbean. She shielded her eyes as she looked at the rose-colored sun that lay low in the sky Wednesday evening.

She sighed and leaned back against Mick's shoulder. He was seated behind her on a rock that jutted into the water at one end of a secluded lagoon, while tropical plants swayed all around them in the soft breeze. A narrow crescent of beach was turning from pure white to creamy pink in the rays of the setting sun.

"This is exactly what I imagined a trip to the Caribbean would be like," Jessica said. "I was going to sit on a sandy beach with a cute guy, watching the setting sun sparkle off the blue water."

"The only sparkle I'm interested in right now is the sparkle in your eyes," Mick replied in a soft, romantic voice. His breath felt warm against the side of her face.

"It's too bad we can't spend the whole week like this," Jessica continued. "I wish we could watch the sunset together every day, and spend time windsurfing and sailing, and dance at the disco, and maybe take a romantic moonlight swim every night. You still haven't seen me in all my bathing suits!"

"Are you sure you can't ditch the brats?" Mick asked. "I'll call in sick for the rest of the week, and we can just concentrate on getting to know each other better."

Jessica turned to him playfully. "And what would you say if I accepted your offer? Would we windsurf into the sunset together right now?"

Mick's eyes widened with what looked like fear, but Jessica knew he was only pretending. She splashed his leg with her foot.

"I guess we can't," she said. "I'd probably get sued for child neglect—or monster neglect. But I was sure close to ditching them today! First, the rotten little urchins messed up my dance performance. Then the boys dyed Maria's hair purple—at least I managed to get the purple off of myself. It washes off of skin easier than it washes out of hair. Anyhow, I thought things couldn't get any worse than that. And then Karen and Suzy wandered off."

"It does sound like an eventful day," Mick said. "I suppose you found everyone in the end?"

"Unfortunately, yes. I had to rescue Suzy from a tree. It was really pretty funny, when I think about it now," Jessica admitted. "But when we got back to the pool, all my good discipline had already worn off. The boys were dismantling all the lounge chairs. And

121

while everyone was trying to stop them, Maria sneaked into the concession stand and ate half the ice cream."

"Let's never have kids," Mick said. "They're too much trouble—even though they would be breathtakingly beautiful, with us as their parents. Think about it, Jessica. Can you imagine what gorgeous blond hair a child of mine would have?"

Jessica caught her breath. *Mick really does love me,* she told herself. He was talking about their future in a perfectly casual tone. Of course, she wasn't anywhere near ready to think about marriage and kids, but it was thrilling to know that the best-looking guy she had ever seen wanted to discuss a long-term relationship.

And of course, she remembered, it didn't hurt her morale any to know that Lila was interested in Mick, too.

"Have you seen Lila around lately?" she asked after a few minutes, trying to keep her tone casual.

"Lila?" he asked. "Oh, I remember—the rich snob with the mousy brown hair. No, I haven't seen Lila in a couple days. What a relief! I just hope I can avoid her for the rest of the week."

"So you don't have plans to go out with her again?"

"I hope not," Mick said. "I'd rather spend every free minute with you. When can you get away again?"

"Probably not until tomorrow night," Jessica said.

"Then tomorrow night it is," Mick said. "I've got the perfect plan. There's going to be a full moon. Let's go for that moonlight swim you mentioned. Meet me on the pier near the yacht club at eight thirty—and wear your sexiest bathing suit."

Jessica smiled. Being with Mick almost made up for everything she hated about this week—the uncomfortable bunks, the nerdy counselors, and the bratty kids. And hearing Mick call Lila "the rich snob with the mousy brown hair" almost made up for her best friend's treachery. Almost.

The red rim of the sun sank beneath the water. Mick placed his hands on Jessica's shoulders and turned her, slowly, to face him. When his lips met hers, Jessica forgot about Lila and about the children she would have to return to soon. A thrill cascaded through her body as Mick gave her a long, tender kiss. At that moment, life was absolutely perfect.

Bruce Patman was the last person in the world that Elizabeth had thought she'd be sitting across from at Guido's pizza parlor Wednesday night. But she couldn't get their earlier conversation out of her mind. Apparently, Bruce couldn't get it out of his mind, either. When he had called to say they needed to talk, Elizabeth had agreed to go for a soda.

"This picture only proves that your father and my mother were married before," Elizabeth said, laying the photograph on the table between them.

"And it proves they're having an affair now!"

Elizabeth shook her head weakly. "Even if they were married years ago, that doesn't necessarily mean . . ." Her voice trailed off.

"Come on, Liz. Face the facts. You saw *Philadelphia Story* today, right? It's the same situation. Katharine Hepburn and Cary Grant had been divorced for years. But in the end, she was as fickle as all women. She threw over the new guy to go back to Cary Grant, her first husband."

"But that's only a movie!" Elizabeth protested, ignoring the slur against women.

"And it's happening the same way now, in real life," Bruce said. "They were in love once. Now they're in love again. First, my parents are getting a divorce. Next, your parents will get a divorce. And then my father will marry your mother." Bruce scowled. "And his social standing will be wrecked forever."

Elizabeth turned to stare at him. "Social standing? Is that all you care about? You're worried because my mother isn't a Vanderbilt or a Carnegie?"

"No," Bruce said. "Of course that's not the only thing I'm worried about."

"Isn't it a little premature to worry about them marrying each other again? Aren't you getting ahead of yourself?"

"And aren't you still sticking your head in the sand? They're having an affair, I tell you." He shook the photograph in her face. "What other proof do you need?"

Elizabeth blinked back tears. "None, I guess," she said softly. "Maybe it really is true. Maybe my mother really is having an affair with your father—her ex-husband."

"Do you want to see a magic trick?" Bobby asked as soon as he emerged from the boys' cabin Thursday morning.

"Get in line with the others and be quiet!" Jessica snapped. "I have to think."

124

"Everybody be quiet!" Maria demanded, shaking her mop of purple curls. "Jessica has to think!"

"I am *not* going to be quiet," Lorenzo said. "Jessica's not my boss."

"Shut up, Lorenzo!" Jessica said sharply. "We're not going through that again. Be quiet so I can come up with a plan."

"Jessica's trying to think of how she can get rid of us," Karen speculated. "She hates us. I bet she wants to take us in the woods and lose us, like Hansel and Gretel."

Suzy folded her chubby arms across her chest. "I won't go," she said. "And you can't make me!"

"It's okay," Gerry Pat said. "I have lots of little pieces of pink and purple material we can use like bread crumbs to make a trail." He held out a grubby hand and slowly opened his fingers. In his palm, Jessica recognized scraps of the polo shirt she had worn yesterday—pink with purple dye stains.

"How did you little rats get hold of my shirt?"

Lorenzo pointed to Bobby and Gerry Pat. "*They* took it from your house last night when you had a date with your loverboy!"

"Oh, *they* took it, did they?" Jessica said vacantly. By now, she was used to Lorenzo egging the other kids on and then denying responsibility. Besides, this morning she had more urgent matters to worry about.

"I don't care about the shirt," she said. "It was ruined, anyhow." She grinned at the disappointed looks on all six faces.

Suddenly, Jessica wondered if the little brats

might make themselves useful, for a change. Maybe they could help her with her problem—if she approached them just right.

"I have to come up with an act for the show this morning," she told them hopefully. "And I don't have any idea what to do."

"You could dance again," Bobby said, giggling.

"Can we be in it?" Suzy asked. "I can be a ballerina."

Jessica pretended to mull it over. "I don't think another dancing act is a good idea. But I guess you can be in it, whatever I decide to do." If she was going to be embarrassed again today, she wasn't going to be embarrassed alone.

"We don't want to be in your show," Lorenzo declared. "It's stupid."

The other children, even Suzy, nodded their heads. As usual, Jessica saw, they were taking their lead from Lorenzo.

"You know," Jessica told him, "everyone says that the other five- and six-year-olds—Lila's kids—are better than you. Their finger painting was better than yours, their arts and crafts didn't fall apart, and they learned all the words to the camp song. Wouldn't you like to show people that you're good at something, too?"

"Those other kids are babies!" Lorenzo objected. "I'm going to bite them when I see them!"

"All right," Jessica said. "You don't have to be in the show, if you really don't have any talents. Of course, everyone will think you're afraid to get onstage in front of all those people. They might say

126

you're a baby, too."

"I am not afraid!" Lorenzo yelled, his face red. "I will, too, do an act in front of all those people!"

"Me, too!" Gerry Pat declared. "I want to be in the show. But what will we do?"

"I can touch my nose with my tongue!" Karen offered.

"I can light matches and set things on fire," Lorenzo said.

"I can catch ants and eat them," Gerry Pat suggested.

Jessica wrinkled her nose. "You kids are just loaded with talent."

Bobby nudged Maria. "This is boring," he said. "Do you want to see a magic trick?"

"That's it!" Jessica whirled to face him. "We'll do a magic act. Bobby can be the magician. I'll be his assistant, and the rest of you can help out wherever we need you. But we only have breakfast time to plan the whole thing. We'll have to work fast."

Suddenly Jessica stopped. She noticed that Lila was engaged in a serious conversation with her charges. The children's napkins were folded on their laps, and they ate with utensils while they listened.

Jessica narrowed her eyes. "That's disgusting." She didn't realize until too late that she had spoken out loud.

Lorenzo's eyes widened with surprise. "They're wimps," he said cautiously, staring at Jessica to gauge her reaction.

For a moment, Jessica felt guilty. After all, she was supposed to be setting an example for these kids.

Then she remembered the thud of her backside hitting the stage during her dance routine the day before. True, it was her own kids who sabotaged her act, but she could still hear Lila's laughter, rising above everyone else's. And it was Lila's fault that she was there in the first place.

"You're right. They are wimps," Jessica said. "And they have a stuck-up counselor who thinks she's better than everybody else."

The children glared at the neat, well-behaved Happy Little Kampers.

Jessica watched her own charges. They were bratty little monsters, all right. But they were *her* little monsters. And for the first time all week, they felt more like allies than enemies. With their help, she was going to do a better act than Lila in this morning's show. She had to.

Jessica refused to be humiliated again.

"We wish to welcome you to Munchkin Land!"

The children finished singing, and Lila smiled broadly at the applause that rang out in the Kiddie Korral Thursday morning.

Lila was proud of her own resourcefulness. As usual, she'd found a way to put her natural charm, her family connections, and her other assets to work for her.

Onstage, Trixie spoke into the microphone in her annoying, singsong voice. "That was wonderful, Lila! It was so clever of you to have the children sing the part of the Munchkins. And you make such a pretty Good Witch of the North!"

Nobody should be that cheerful at eight in the morning, Lila thought, stifling a yawn.

Of course, she admitted to herself, Trixie was right. Lila's act had been fantastic. The song from *The Wizard of Oz* had been a good choice. The tape had been playing in the arts-and-crafts area the evening before; all Lila had to do was urge the children to sing along while they worked on their pasta-and-dried-bean mosaics. They had learned quickly.

Even the full-skirted formal she was wearing had been easy to come by. An assurance of future baby-sitting opportunities was all it took to buy Renata's cooperation—Renata worked in the formalwear shop at the adult Club Paradise. The rest of Lila's part had been even easier. She had waved her wand a few times onstage, welcomed everyone to the Land of Oz, and then let the kids sing.

Now it was over, and Lila was resting on her well-deserved laurels. At least she could count on her children to behave themselves. Lila leaned back in her chair and closed her eyes as the applause died down.

The two nerdy little counselors, Howard and Harold, were noisily setting up the stage for their performance, when Lila heard a voice from behind her.

"Your act was great, Lila!"

Lila rolled her eyes, and then turned to greet Julia with a gracious smile. She really didn't want to talk to the girl—after all, somebody might think they were friends. But there were a few free minutes between acts, and Lila couldn't think of an excuse to ignore her.

Julia didn't notice Lila's lack of enthusiasm. "I mean it, Lila. You have a real gift for working with children. I bet you're planning to be a teacher when you grow up."

Lila wanted to laugh. Instead, she raised her eyebrows and stared haughtily at the other counselor.

"As luck would have it," Lila said dryly, "I have other gifts, as well. But I have to admit I've surprised myself this week by turning out to be an outstanding teacher. I never would have thought I could take six *children*"—she wrinkled her nose—"and in such a short time, turn them into useful *people*."

Julia laughed. "You're so together, Lila. You even have a sense of humor! If I didn't know any better, I'd think you *hated* kids!"

"Imagine that."

"There's only one more performance after Harold and Howard," Julia said after a pause. "It's that self-centered Jessica Wakefield. After her klutz act yesterday, I don't know how she can even show her face!"

Lila had to quell an urge to come to Jessica's defense. She shook her head, surprised at her own weakness. *I don't owe Jessica Wakefield a thing!* she thought.

Lila smiled serenely. "I'm sure Jessica Wakefield won't present any competition at all."

Chapter 10

Gerry Pat hurried across the stage, trembling with excitement and self-importance. He stood on his toes to speak into the microphone.

"Ladies and gentlemen—dudes and dudettes—here is Bobby the Magnificent!"

The audience applauded as Bobby walked onstage, a plastic rain poncho rippling behind him like a cape. He wore a tall black hat made out of cardboard and carried a stick for a magic wand. At Bobby's insistence, Jessica had drawn a black mustache onto his face with her eyeliner pencil, though she thought it looked silly, with his fair skin and blond hair.

Jessica followed, wearing her sequined top and a black miniskirt. The Kiddie Korral wasn't exactly the fast-lane setting she had envisioned when she packed the outfit, but at least she was getting the chance to wear it.

Gerry Pat was supposed to let Bobby have the microphone. Instead, he kept speaking. "And I present the magician's helper, Jessica the Klutz!"

Jessica clenched her teeth to keep from screaming at him. She kept a smile plastered onto her face, for the audience, but the eyes she turned on Gerry Pat were menacing. "If you try another stunt like that," she whispered, careful to stay out of range of the microphone, "I'll tell Lorenzo that your nickname at home is The Pudge."

Gerry Pat's face turned so pale that his freckles stood out like Christmas lights. "I'll be good!" he whispered. Then he scurried off stage, casting pleading looks in Jessica's direction.

Bobby nudged Jessica. "*I'm* the star!" he reminded her, speaking too close to the microphone. The audience tittered.

The performance was only supposed to last a few minutes, but Jessica already knew that it would seem a lot longer. Offstage, Lorenzo was whispering something to Gerry Pat. Lorenzo had a mischievous sneer on his face; Gerry Pat kept glancing at Jessica with terror in his eyes. Onstage, Bobby had already forgotten his first line and was staring out at the audience with wide eyes.

"Bobby the Magnificent needs a volunteer from the audience," Jessica said into the microphone for him.

Suzy jumped up from her seat in the first row and waved her hand in the air, right on cue.

Bobby pulled a deck of cards out of his backpack. "Pick a card, any card!" he commanded after Suzy joined him onstage. Suzy tentatively selected one.

"Not that card, you dope!" Bobby whispered, still too close to the microphone. "You're supposed to pick the card with the little mark on it!"

"Well, I forgot," Suzy said aloud. Again, the microphone picked up every word.

The audience laughed, and Suzy stared at the campers and counselors uncertainly before joining in.

Jessica wanted to die. The children were doing their best to embarrass her again—in front of everyone. In front of Lila.

But this laughter didn't sound like ridicule. In fact, it sounded as if the audience was actually enjoying this—as if they thought Suzy and Bobby were just innocent, funny little children.

How naive! Jessica thought. Surely by now, everyone realized that Suzy and Bobby, like the rest of the gang, were mutant monsters out of a horror movie, in disguise.

"Try it again, Suzy," Bobby hissed. Then he turned to the audience. "Now the little girl will pick another card. She won't let me see it. But then I'll be able to tell which card she picked. Because I'm Bobby the Magnificent—and I'm magic."

Suzy selected the marked card and handed it to Jessica, who showed it to the audience, keeping it turned away from Bobby. The five of spades—*no surprise there,* thought Jessica as she replaced the card in the deck.

When Suzy tried to shuffle the cards, the deck erupted from her hands and cards flew all over the stage. The surprised look on Suzy's face drew more laughter from the audience.

"It worked this morning," Suzy confided into the microphone, to a round of applause.

Bobby nudged her away. "This is *my* act!" he said. "Now Jessica the Klutzy will play fifty-two-card pick-up!"

Jessica didn't care what Bobby called her. She just wanted to get this over with. She bent down to scoop up a handful of cards. As she did, Bobby the Magnificent filled the time by pretending to pull some colorful scarves out of Suzy's ear.

"Don't pull too fast, Bobby the Maggot!" Suzy said. "They'll see that the scarves are really under my shirt!"

The audience howled.

Jessica sighed. The children were making a disaster out of the magic show, but everyone thought they were doing it on purpose. They thought it was supposed to be a comedy! Jessica didn't know what else to do, so she played along. She saw the marked card, facedown under Bobby's foot, and tapped on his sneaker with an exaggerated motion.

"Bobby the Magnificent has used his foot to find Suzy's card!" Jessica called loudly. "Bobby can use his magic powers to read it through his shoe!"

Bobby closed his eyes for a moment and made a humming sound into the mike. "Five of spades!" he announced finally.

"How did you do that?" Suzy asked.

"I'm magic, remember?" Bobby said. "Your turn's over, Suzy. You go away so I can pick Maria and Karen now."

"Can't you pull more scarves out of my ear?"

The audience laughed harder.

Jessica didn't understand. These children were not funny—they were monsters. But for some reason, people thought little kids were cute anytime they weren't being destructive. Jessica's act was turning out to be the hit of the morning.

"Bobby the Magnificent needs two more volunteers from the audience," Jessica said into the microphone.

Bobby pointed his stick at Karen and Maria in the front row, but Suzy objected. "I'm not going to leave! I want Bobby the Maggot to make me disappear."

"Aw, let the little girl stay!" called someone from the audience. Suzy smiled at the unexpected support.

Karen and Maria jumped to their feet in the front row. "We want to be famous, too!"

"I can do something Bobby can't do!" Karen boasted, turning to the audience. She touched her tongue to the tip of her nose.

Maria proudly yanked off the cap Jessica had made her wear. "And I have purple hair!"

"I'm doing the trick with Suzy!" Bobby yelled. "If you don't sit down, I'll turn you into ants, and Gerry Pat will eat you!"

The audience loved it. The girls sat down.

Jessica wished all six children would disappear.

"Now, for my grand finale," Bobby announced, "I'm going to make Suzy disappear."

Suzy grinned triumphantly as Lorenzo and Gerry Pat trooped onstage to help with the trick. Jessica stared suspiciously at the two boys. They were up to something. Lorenzo's smile was too broad, and Gerry Pat kept stealing frightened glances at Jessica.

"Now you see her!" Bobby yelled, gesturing toward Suzy. The little girl put her finger in her mouth, suddenly confused about what she was supposed to do. Lorenzo and Gerry Pat held up a vinyl tablecloth they had borrowed from the Kiddie Kabana. Suzy ducked behind the tablecloth, and Jessica heard Lorenzo giving her whispered instructions as Bobby recited the magic words.

"Abracadabra! Hocus pocus!"

Jessica hadn't heard Lorenzo's instructions. And she couldn't see behind the tablecloth from where she was standing. But Jessica knew the plan. The girls who were "disappearing" were supposed to run straight to the back of the stage while the tablecloth was hiding them. Then they would jump off the back of the stage and hide behind it as Bobby said the magic words, until he was ready to make them appear again.

Lorenzo and Gerry Pat dropped the tablecloth. Suzy was gone.

"Now you don't see her!" Bobby said, obviously proud of himself. The audience applauded good-naturedly as the other boys lifted the tablecloth again.

Now it was time to make Suzy reappear. Bobby recited more magic words, and Lorenzo and Gerry Pat dropped the tablecloth. The audience became silent. Suzy was not there.

"Gee, I'm really good at this!" Bobby exclaimed with a grin.

The audience applauded, laughing. Jessica rolled her eyes. The three boys must have cooked this up just to upset her. She wasn't about to give them the satisfaction—she just shrugged. "I suppose she'll turn up sooner or later," she said to the crowd.

Karen stood up in the front row. "Can I have her Ninja Turtles if she doesn't?"

Their time was up, so Jessica led the children off the stage. Unbelievably, the audience gave them a standing ovation.

There's no accounting for taste, Jessica thought. But she saw that Lila looked away when Jessica and her charges passed by.

Suzy joined Jessica and the others at their seats a few minutes later. "I had to go to the bathroom," she explained loudly. The rows of people seated near them erupted in laughter. "Why did you finish without me? Lorenzo said you would wait."

"Well, we didn't," Jessica whispered harshly. She softened at the little girl's downcast expression. "Don't worry, Suzy. The audience loved you."

Suzy smiled happily.

Jessica was beginning to feel better about the performance, as well. It felt good to know that the audience had liked her act better than Lila's. And now that the ordeal was over, Jessica had to admit that it had been funny. Unfortunately, Jessica didn't have anyone to share her triumph with. She would have loved to tell Mick all about it on the beach this afternoon. He had invited her out, but she couldn't arrange to get away.

For a moment, Jessica wished that she was still speaking to Lila, so that they could laugh about it together. But that was impossible, she reminded herself. She was mad at Lila. At least Lila hadn't had the satisfaction of seeing Jessica humiliated again. But stealing the stage from Lila was only a minor part of Jessica's revenge. Stealing Mick was much more important.

Luckily, Jessica thought, *I seem to have succeeded in both areas.*

"Are you all right, Liz?" Enid asked as Elizabeth climbed into the backseat of Olivia's car early Thursday afternoon. "You look a little down."

"I'm fine," Elizabeth assured her. "It's this horrible heat. I feel like a french fry." She fanned herself with her hand.

"Is Bruce still being a pain in the neck?" Enid asked.

"If Bruce weren't a pain in the neck, he'd have no personality at all," Olivia said.

Elizabeth forced a laugh. "That's for sure," she said. But lately, Bruce was beginning to feel almost like an ally. With Jessica away, Bruce was the only person she could talk to about her mother's secret past.

"So is he still bugging you about those crazy fantasies of his?" Enid persisted.

"Not too much."

Enid turned around in her seat. "Liz, I hope you're not falling for Bruce's stories about your mother and his father."

Elizabeth smiled weakly. "Of course not. My mother isn't like that."

Elizabeth didn't feel comfortable talking about the wedding photograph of her mother and Mr.

138

Patman. Not yet. Not until she felt that she knew something more about the situation.

Enid and Olivia exchanged a concerned glance. But Elizabeth didn't think they would push her if it was clear she didn't feel like talking. She decided a change of subject was in order. "I'm looking forward to today's movie," she said brightly. "I've never seen *His Girl Friday*. I know Cary Grant and Rosalind Russell star in it. What's it about?"

"You'll love it," Enid said. "I'm surprised you haven't seen it before, since it's set in a newspaper office. Rosalind Russell plays a reporter and Cary Grant is her editor. She has to work with him on a major story. And he's her ex-husband."

Elizabeth slumped in her seat. It was going to be a long afternoon.

"Watch out!" called a sexy-sounding voice. Jessica ducked as a Frisbee zoomed by her head. A tall, exotic-looking boy with dark hair and a great tan smiled apologetically.

"This is the life!" Jessica said under her breath.

This was what the Caribbean was supposed to be. The sparkling sand was warm on her bare feet, the blue-green water was the same color as her eyes, and the guys on the beach were eyeing her new, skimpy bikini. She walked slowly to give them all a chance to notice her. Later, she would decide which ones she wanted to get to know better—if she didn't run into Mick. For now, it was enough just to be here on the beach on a glorious Thursday afternoon, instead of back in Munchkin Land with her Happy Little Monsters.

Jessica was still disappointed about having to turn down Mick's invitation to spend the afternoon on the beach with him. At the time, she hadn't been able to think of anyone who might take care of the children. But at the last minute, Marcy and Charles had agreed to watch them. So now Jessica was free, but there had been no answer at Mick's phone number. So Jessica had headed to the beach, hoping Mick had come by himself.

She scanned the crowded beach, inspecting the array of tanned, well-muscled bodies in swim trunks. Even if Mick wasn't here, Jessica was sure she could manage to amuse herself somehow.

"Jessica!" somebody called.

It was a male voice, but it didn't sound like Mick. *Who else do I know in Montego Bay?* Jessica pushed her sunglasses up on her forehead to get a better look. "Well, if it isn't Larry the Lifeguard!" she exclaimed. "I didn't know they ever let you away from Kiddie Paradise."

"Kiddie Chaos is more like it," Larry said, grimacing. "But occasionally they unchain me from my lifeguard chair and let me spend an afternoon in real Paradise. What about you? I thought you were permanently stuck with those six little scorpions you call children."

"The monster brigade? I was dying to get away from them today. But, Larry, I could've sworn that you hated me. Every time I come near you, I get the feeling you want to turn and bolt."

"It wasn't you I wanted to bolt from."

"Is a big, strong lifeguard like you scared of a few darling little children?"

"Of course not. But I'm terrified of that six-pack

of mutant Martians you're supposed to be taming."

Jessica appraised him. Along with having obvious good sense when it came to children, Larry was really rather good-looking. Like most lifeguards—and Jessica had looked· at a lot of lifeguards—Larry had a great body. He was tall, with broad shoulders and a wonderful tan. He also had wavy brown hair, a strong chin, and sparkling hazel eyes.

Of course, Jessica reminded herself, *Mick is the guy I really care about.* But Mick wasn't here.

"You know, Jessica," Larry said, "the sun is intense here, and you don't have any lotion on your back. Can I help you with that? You wouldn't want to get sunburned."

Jessica smiled. Larry would do just fine.

A few minutes later, Jessica was lying on her stomach while Larry rubbed suntan lotion between her shoulder blades. "Make sure you get the backs of my arms," she told him.

"I wouldn't miss the backs of your arms for anything, my dear."

"When you're finished there, would you do me a teeny-tiny favor? Would you get us something to drink? It took me so long to arrange the straps on this bikini top to get my tan lines in just the right places. I'd hate to move now and have to do it all over again."

"Sounds like a worthy cause," Larry said, twisting the cap on the tube of suntan lotion. "What do you want me to bring you?"

"I don't know," Jessica murmured sleepily, relishing the feel of the warm sun baking her bare skin. "Surprise me."

Chapter 11

Mick's arm around Lila's shoulders gave her a warm, tingly feeling inside. So did the jealous stares of the other girls. Lila laughed aloud, happy to be strolling on the beach on a perfect Thursday afternoon. She was wearing a skimpy bikini, and she had the best-looking guy in the Caribbean as her date.

"That bistro was excellent, Mick," she said, admiring the way his golden hair reflected the warm sunlight. "Those local paintings all over the walls were so quaint! And I couldn't believe the incredible view of the bay."

"I knew you'd like it," Mick said. "It's one of the best spots on the island for lunch, but it's too special to take just anyone to. Of course, you're not just anyone."

You're darn right I'm not, Lila thought. Unfortunately, some guys never seemed to catch on to that. But Mick was different. From the moment they met, Mick had known instinctively that Lila Fowler was used to special treatment. And he had been eager to give her the attention she deserved.

"You know, Lila, I'm going to miss you," Mick said. "It's already Thursday. I can't believe you're leaving on Saturday."

"Me neither," Lila said. "It's too bad I've had to waste so much of this week keeping an eye on those little pests. Personally, I've always believed that children should be neither seen nor heard until they're at least thirteen. Sixteen, if they're boys."

Mick laughed. "Sounds sexist to me."

"Just a fact of life," Lila said in a superior tone. "Everybody knows girls mature faster than boys—well, in most cases," she added, thinking of Jessica.

"What happens after boys turn sixteen? Do you have any use for them then?"

"Oh, I can think of one or two uses."

She looked up into Mick's eyes, surprised, as always, at their brilliant shade of blue. Mick smiled, leaned over, and kissed her slowly on the lips.

Lila's mind went blank. She felt as if she were going to melt into the sand. She was annoyed with herself for having no willpower at all when it came to Mick. At the same time, she didn't want him ever to stop.

A loud male voice brought her back to her senses.

"Way to go, Mick!" Larry, the dark-haired lifeguard from Club Paradise, was sauntering toward them with two sodas in his hands and a big grin on his face.

"As usual, Larry, your timing leaves something to be desired," Mick complained.

Larry ignored him. Instead, his hazel eyes lingered over Lila's bikini. "Have you ever thought about being a lifeguard, Lila? From what I just saw, it looks like you show a real talent for mouth-to-mouth resuscitation."

"She certainly does," Mick agreed in a soft voice.

Lila stared into Mick's brilliant blue eyes. "Only with the right patient."

"Speaking of patients, I think I'm going to be sick!" Larry said.

"You're just jealous, pal—of my looks *and* my girl," Mick told him, running a hand through his silky golden hair. "You and every other guy on the beach is jealous."

"Jealous? No way!" Larry said. "At this very moment, there's a gorgeous girl in a very skimpy bikini, waiting for yours truly to rub more suntan lotion on all those hard-to-reach spots. We've got our own little corner of the beach staked out. Would you two lovebirds like to join us—or would you rather be alone?"

"Hi, honey, I'm home!" Larry called gleefully.

Jessica was still lying on her stomach on her beach towel, facing the ocean. "Great," she began. "I'm dying for a drink." She turned her head, shading her eyes with her hand. "What did you bring—"

Jessica stopped, speechless. Next to Larry stood Mick, looking as gorgeous as always, especially in his skimpy bathing suit. And next to Mick was Lila.

"Hello, Jessica," Mick said in a formal tone.

Oh no, Jessica thought. *He's mad at me for being here with another guy.* As soon as she had a minute alone with Mick, Jessica decided, she would explain that she had tried to call him but couldn't get through. He would understand. He had to.

"I guess you know Lila, too," Larry said, handing Jessica her drink.

Jessica sat up to face Lila. "We've met," she said coldly.

How dare she? Jessica thought indignantly. Lila knew that Jessica was dating Mick, yet she bugged him to take her out all the time. It was bad enough that Lila would try to mess up the only good thing about Jessica's week here. But Lila was putting Mick in a very awkward position. She knew perfectly well that Mick couldn't turn down a date with his boss's niece.

Now Lila was standing there in her hundred-dollar bikini, gloating. To make matters worse, she was hanging on to Mick's arm as if she owned him. Well, Jessica could be just as cool as Lila. Especially since she knew who Mick really liked best.

"Hi, Jessica," Lila said in her most syrupy voice. "That's a cute bikini you're wearing. Which designer is it a *copy* of?"

Jessica clenched her fist behind her back, but she smiled graciously. "Oh, this old thing? It's just something I picked up somewhere. But I just love *your* bikini, Li. I can tell that it's brand new—I guess all of your others were getting too small."

Jessica was gratified to see a flicker of anger cross Lila's usually serene face.

Larry didn't seem to notice the tension between the two girls. But Mick's reaction was hard to gauge.

145

He had turned his back and was busily spreading out Lila's beach towel.

Poor Mick, Jessica thought. *This must be so uncomfortable for him.* She promised herself that she would find a way to pull him aside, soon. She had to tell him that she understood why he had to spend time with Lila when he'd rather be with her.

"Who's up for a swim?" Larry asked.

"Absolutely not, Olivia," Elizabeth said, treading water in the Wakefield swimming pool. The girls had just returned from seeing the Thursday matinee, *His Girl Friday.* "Rosalind Russell was engaged to marry Ralph Bellamy, for goodness' sake! I don't care if Cary Grant was her ex-husband. It would be wrong for her to dump her fiancé to go back to him."

"Chill out, Liz!" Enid said, looking at her curiously from the inflatable raft she was floating on. "It's only a movie."

Liz managed a weak laugh. "Sorry," she said. "I guess I'm getting carried away. I think the heat has fried my brain."

Elizabeth submerged, as if to cool off. Underwater, she scolded herself silently. She would have to keep better control of her emotions.

Elizabeth still hadn't told Enid and Olivia about the wedding photograph of her mother and Henry Patman. She resurfaced near Enid's raft and smiled at her best friend. "All right," she said. "I think I'm relatively normal again. We can go back to having a nice, friendly, out-and-out war."

"If water is all it takes to cure temporary insanity,"

Enid suggested, "somebody ought to give Bruce Patman a good dunking."

"It won't work," Olivia said, sitting on the edge of the pool. "Bruce's insanity is the permanent kind."

"This week's matinees at the Plaza Theatre are sure getting popular," Enid said. "The place was really packed today. Did you notice Amy and Caroline in the audience? That's the first time they've come."

"I wouldn't have pegged Amy and Caroline as the type to go for old romance movies," Elizabeth replied, glad of the change in subject. "But I guess everyone's getting pretty bored this week."

"I still don't get it, Liz," Enid said. "After *Casablanca,* you said it was all right for Ingrid Bergman to leave her husband to go back to Humphrey Bogart— *her one true love.* As I remember, *I* was the one pushing marriage and commitment."

"Does your change of heart have anything to do with Bruce's recent adventures in slander?" Olivia asked gently. "You're not still worried about his paranoid delusions, are you, Liz?"

"Of course not," Elizabeth said, a little too loudly. Olivia and Enid both looked at her skeptically. "It has nothing to do with Bruce. I've just reconsidered my views. I was wrong, and Enid was right."

"Stick with me, kid," Enid urged. "You'll learn a lot!"

Elizabeth swam under the inflatable raft and overturned it, sending Enid into the water with a huge splash. Enid surfaced and splashed Elizabeth. Elizabeth ducked, and the cascade of water hit Olivia instead.

"Of course, I was right about *Casablanca,*" Enid

said thoughtfully a few minutes later. "But I'm not sure the same rule holds in this movie. In *His Girl Friday*, Russell and Bellamy didn't have a marriage yet—only an engagement. If you're going to decide you've picked the wrong guy, isn't that the best time to change your mind?"

"Maybe," Elizabeth said. "But an engagement is a commitment too. Should she break off that relationship to get back together with Grant, just because she was married to Grant in the past?"

"But that's not the only reason," Olivia reminded. "What happened to your 'one true love' theory? Doesn't that count for anything?"

Elizabeth held on to the side of the pool and considered the question. "I'm not sure," she said. "I think I still believe it. But is there any reason why your *first* love has to be your one true love? Maybe Ralph Bellamy was Rosalind Russell's true love—not Cary Grant."

"No way!" Olivia protested. "How could any woman in her right mind be in love with Bellamy over Grant?"

Elizabeth continued as if Olivia hadn't spoken. "And who's to say that Bogart was Bergman's one true love? Maybe she really did love her husband. Maybe her relationship with Bogart was only an infatuation—because he was glamorous and exciting . . ."

"I don't know, Liz," Enid said. "You sound like someone who's trying pretty hard to convince herself."

Jessica stepped on a slimy rock as a wave buffeted

her body. She grabbed for Larry's arm. She regained her footing without falling face-first into the hip-deep water—but only after accidentally splashing Lila.

Jessica grinned. Lila was never at her best when her hair was dripping.

"Watch it, Jess," Mick cautioned. "You almost got my hair wet."

"You girls are great," Larry said. "So many girls are chicken when it comes to the ocean. But not you two. Do you know that some girls are afraid of jellyfish?"

Jessica's eyes widened. *Jellyfish?*

For a moment, Jessica wished she and Lila were friends again. If they were friends, they could agree that jellyfish were not good swimming companions. Then they could retreat to their towels on the sand to work on their tans and talk about boys.

Jessica noticed that Lila had practically vaulted onto Mick's shoulders at the first mention of jellyfish. Mick didn't seem to mind.

He is really a good actor, Jessica thought, marvelling at yet another talent of Mick's. Maybe Lila really believed that Mick liked her. Luckily, Jessica knew the truth.

Suddenly, a huge fan of water splattered Jessica from her hair down to her bikini bottoms. Lila had splashed her.

This was war.

Larry was also dripping. "We're not going to let them get away with that, are we?" he asked, his hazel eyes twinkling. He leaned over, and Jessica climbed onto his shoulders.

"The couple who falls apart first loses!" Larry exclaimed.

Mick laughed, showing straight, white teeth. "It'll be a fight to the finish!" he said. "Two beautiful beach bunnies, locked in hand-to-hand combat to hang on to their men."

Jessica wished that Mick didn't look so happy about the prospect of the girls trying to knock each other into the ocean. She dismissed the disloyal thought and turned her attention to Lila. The enemy.

Lila had dashed her dreams of a glorious Caribbean holiday. Lila had laughed when Jessica was publicly humiliated during her modern dance routine. And Lila was trying to steal the best-looking boy Jessica had ever dated.

Jessica narrowed her eyes at her former friend as the two guys began circling each other. Jessica felt a little unsteady, sitting on Larry's shoulders as he rocked back and forth with the waves. Suddenly, a bigger wave thudded against Larry's body. Jessica lurched to one side.

Then Larry regained his footing, and Jessica took a deep breath. She refused to give Lila the satisfaction of seeing her topple into the water.

Another wave crashed. Mick rocked forward, bringing Lila within arm's reach. Jessica tried to knock her off Mick's shoulders. Mick turned to one side. Jessica's hand glanced harmlessly off Lila's shoulder.

Larry stepped closer, and Lila threw herself against Jessica's shoulder. Jessica, beginning to fall, grabbed for Larry's wet hair.

"Hey!" he yelled, stepping away from Mick and Lila.

"You might as well give up now, Jessica," Lila said coldly. "You're not going to get me away from Mick."

Mick began running with her toward the deeper water.

"Sure we will!" Larry called, following them. "We'll get you off his shoulders and into the water with all those jellyfish—if it's the last thing Jessica does."

"Thanks, Larry," Jessica said, rolling her eyes. She glared at Lila, dead serious, as Mick turned to face Larry and Jessica. "But he's right, Lila. You might as well give up right now, because this is one war you're not going to win."

Lila lunged forward and slapped Jessica's arm, hard. Jessica rocked wildly and tightened her grip on Larry's neck. When another wave hit, both boys lurched. Mick fell toward Larry. Jessica grabbed Lila's left leg and tried to push her off Mick's shoulders. Lila freed her leg and kicked Jessica in the kneecap.

As Mick whirled to face another incoming wave, Lila's long hair flew out around her shoulders. Jessica grabbed a handful of it and yanked. Lila swung out with one arm and batted Jessica in the ear.

Jessica looked up in time to see a wall of water bearing down on both couples. As she tumbled into the water, Jessica caught a glimpse of Lila catapulting headfirst over Mick's shining hair.

"I heard Mrs. Wakefield was away on business," Amy said to Elizabeth's father at dinner

151

Thursday night. "When will she be back?"

It had been easy to get an invitation to eat at the Wakefield house with Elizabeth and her father. Amy had shown up at the front door at six thirty, pretending she needed to talk to Elizabeth about her family biography. Mr. Wakefield had immediately invited her to dinner. Now she just had to wait for the perfect moment to get him talking about Jessamyn.

"We're kind of playing it by ear," Mr. Wakefield admitted, helping himself to some cottage cheese. "She had hoped to be gone for only a day or two, but the project is more complex than anyone expected. She'll be home for the weekend. But I wouldn't be surprised if she has to travel again soon."

"That's too bad," Elizabeth said. Her voice was low-key, but Amy thought she looked as if she'd been wounded.

"Don't worry about your English paper, honey," Mr. Wakefield told her. "You can talk to her Saturday for sure. Or you could interview her by phone."

Elizabeth gave him a weak smile.

"So how's your paper going, Amy?" Mr. Wakefield asked. "Elizabeth told me she's giving you some research tips."

Amy took a long drink of lemonade. "It's coming along," she lied. "But my family's not nearly as interesting as yours, Mr. Wakefield. For instance, Elizabeth was telling me about her own great-great-grandmother, Jessamyn. Was she really a circus bareback rider?"

"She sure was," he said, leaning back in his chair. "I don't know the whole story, but Alice has told me a

152

little bit about her. Jessamyn grew up in Minnesota. When she was sixteen, she ran away in the middle of the night to join the circus."

"She didn't even tell her family she was going?"

"Not a word," he said.

"Did she already know how to ride bareback, or did they teach her after she joined the circus?"

"I'm not sure," Mr. Wakefield said, "but I think she had a horse, so she must have known how to ride."

Elizabeth hardly seemed to be listening, Amy noticed. She was staring at her plate, picking at her sliced tomatoes with a fork. *Maybe she misses Todd,* Amy decided. *The two of them are practically joined at the hip when he's around.*

"What else do you know about Jessamyn?" Amy asked Elizabeth's father.

"Not a lot," he said. "Alice's mother once told me that Jessamyn and her twin sister, Elisabeth, were a lot like our Jessica and Elizabeth. Jessamyn had a wild, impulsive streak. Elisabeth was quieter and more serious, though I remember hearing that she was very brave."

"I heard that Elisabeth died in a horseback-riding accident. What did Jessamyn do after that?"

"I'm not sure. But much later, she lived in Detroit and had another set of twins. Why all this interest, Amy? Aren't you supposed to research your own family?"

Amy shrugged. "I guess all this talk has made me want to learn more about everyone's family history. And as I said, your family is so much more interesting than mine."

Jessica fingered her sore shoulder as she stepped onto the pier Thursday night. She wondered if she had a bruise. Lila didn't have to hit her so hard!

She chuckled in spite of herself. She and Lila must have been quite a spectacle that afternoon, trying to knock each other into the surf.

Jessica had managed to get Mick alone for a minute after the four had emerged from the water. He had apologized for being stuck with Lila again. And Jessica had explained that she had run into Larry only by accident. She smiled when she remembered how relieved Mick had looked.

"Are we still on for tonight?" she had asked.

"Tonight?"

"You know, our moonlight swim off the pier."

"Of course we're still on," Mick had said. She loved the way he had peeked over her shoulder to be sure Lila wasn't looking—before he blew her a discreet kiss. "Nothing could keep me from my moonlight swim with a golden mermaid."

That was when Jessica had decided which bathing suit to wear that night—the shiny gold bikini that Elizabeth had said looked more like a headband. "A golden mermaid," Jessica whispered as she walked along the pier. She liked the sound of the words. Of course, she admitted to herself with a sheepish smile, she liked the sound of almost anything Mick said.

Jessica stopped halfway down the long, wide pier and breathed deeply of the salt-scented air. She gazed out over the water. In the west, a faint rose-colored stain still tinged the sky, left over from the spectacular sunset. But mostly the night was dark blue and gold. To Jessica's left, the shadowy shapes of boats bobbed silently around the yacht club. Stars poked golden pinpricks through the midnight-blue sky overhead. All around her, Jessica heard the soft lapping of the waves against the pier.

A sea gull flew overhead, screaming, and Jessica focused her thoughts. Mick was meeting her at the end of the pier. In fact, she thought she was a few minutes late, as usual. Mick was probably there now, waiting for her. Wasn't that a figure she saw seated up ahead?

She approached quietly.

"Mick?" she asked.

"Jessica?"

The seated figure jumped up and faced her angrily.

"Lila Fowler, haven't you screwed up my week enough?" Jessica cried in exasperation. "Why are you trying to wreck my date, too?"

"Your date? What about my date? You must have known I was supposed to meet Mick here ten minutes ago. It would be just like you, Jessica, to follow me here and try to come between me and Mick. You're just jealous that he likes me and not you."

Jessica laughed coldly. "Wrong. I'm the one Mick is in love with. He's only humoring you because your uncle is his boss."

"Jess, you really ought to see a specialist about these fantasies of yours. Mick only goes out with you because you're so pushy. He called you a dumb blonde!"

If there was one thing that made Jessica's blood

boil, it was being called a dumb blonde. Before she could think about it, her right hand swung out and slapped Lila across the face.

Jessica didn't hit her hard, but Lila hadn't expected the sudden attack. She lost her footing and toppled off the edge of the pier. As she fell, she grabbed Jessica and pulled her down, too.

As soon as Jessica hit the cold water, she realized what she had done. She could have seriously hurt Lila. "Sorry," Jessica murmured when Lila's head bobbed to the surface next to her. "I didn't mean to knock you into the water. But you should know better than to call me a dumb blonde. You know how I get when someone calls me that!"

"I didn't call you that," Lila said, treading water. "Mick did."

"No, he didn't," Jessica protested. "Mick wouldn't say something like that—certainly not to you. Why, he told me himself that you're a mousy brunette and a stuck-up snob."

"No, he didn't," Lila said. "If he felt that way, he wouldn't be going out with me."

"I told you, he only goes out with you because he's afraid of annoying your uncle. He said so himself."

Lila put a wet hand on Jessica's arm. "Did he really?"

Jessica was confused by the strange tone in Lila's voice. "Yes, he did," she insisted. "And he called you a stuck-up snob."

"Don't you get it, Jess? Mick told me he didn't want to go out with you. He said he was dating you only because regular staff are supposed to be friendly to the temporary counselors."

Jessica's eyes widened. "He said that?"

"Over and over again."

Jessica pulled herself onto the ladder at the end of the pier and climbed up, with Lila following behind. They sat side by side with their legs dangling over the edge.

"I smell something fishy," Jessica said finally, "and it has nothing to do with the ocean."

"I can't believe he did this to us," Lila fumed, pounding her fist against the pier. "Mick dated both of us at the same time. We really liked him. And the whole time, he was lying to us both!"

"He could get away with it because he knew we weren't speaking to each other," Jessica realized aloud. "Think about it. Mick gets to spend a week juggling the two best-looking girls on the staff—and probably bragging to his friends about how he's putting one over on both of us."

"Nobody makes a fool out of Lila Fowler," Lila said through clenched teeth. She turned to Jessica. "Nobody does that to either of us."

"What a slimeball!" Jessica screeched, realizing the magnitude of Mick's actions. "How dare he?" She jumped up and yelled, "Mick Myers is a complete and total jerk!"

As the echo died down, Jessica sat next to Lila again, feeling a little foolish but strangely gratified.

"That's for sure!" came a thin, female voice from the direction of the yacht club.

Lila and Jessica looked at each other and burst out laughing.

"Mick is going to pay for what he did," Lila

said. "He's going to pay for it, big time."

"But how?" Jessica asked.

"We're leaving on Saturday," Lila said. "That only gives us tomorrow to come up with a plan. We can do it—if we work together." Lila stopped speaking and looked at Jessica uncertainly.

Jessica hesitated. She thought about the way Lila had deceived her into coming on this trip in the first place. It was Lila's fault that she had to put up with the kids, the uncomfortable cabins, the nerdy counselors, and the humiliating morning shows.

But none of that could compare with what Mick had done. It wasn't Lila's fault that Mick had turned out to be a creep. He had done it to both of them. And now they would get their revenge. Together.

Jessica clapped Lila on the shoulder. "You're on!" she said. "There's no point in being mad at each other anymore, now that we've found somebody who really deserves it! But it's got to be something awful. Something that will humiliate him in public and make him think twice before he ever tries to pull anything like this again."

"We'll come up with a plan," Lila said confidently. "And it'll be a terrific one. With you and me working together, how can we miss?"

Chapter 12

Julia opened one eye and glanced at her travel alarm clock. It was after ten o'clock on Thursday night— pretty late for three of the counselors to still be out. Marcy was in her bunk, reading. But Julia hadn't seen Jessica, Lila, or the other counselor, Anne, all evening. Now somebody was approaching the bunkhouse, talking in loud, excited tones.

Only Jessica could be that loud and obnoxious, she thought.

The door opened. So did Marcy's mouth. Jessica and Lila hurried in, chatting as if they were the best of friends. Julia couldn't help being disappointed. Jessica and Lila had been glaring at each other across the bunkhouse all week. What had happened to change their relationship? Now Lila would never join forces with her against Jessica.

I should have known better than to trust a girl that attractive, Julia thought. She stayed under the covers and pretended to be asleep. She always learned more when people thought she wasn't listening.

Marcy glanced from Jessica to Lila. "What's up with you two?" she asked. "I thought you hated each other."

Jessica smiled. "Not anymore. That was all a big misunderstanding."

"That's right," said Lila. "Now we're a team again."

"Too bad you couldn't have made up earlier in the week," Marcy commented. "You could have had a lot more fun here."

Julia gave up on keeping a low profile. "Too bad you couldn't have made up earlier in the day," she complained. "I could have had a lot more sleep tonight."

"Marcy, we need your help," Jessica begged, ignoring Julia. "You once told me Mick Myers was trouble. You said you had personal experience with him. Tell us about it."

"Mick?" Marcy asked, looking from Jessica's face to Lila's. "He's the last topic I thought the two of you would want to talk about together."

"You're asking the wrong person," Julia said, sitting up. "*I'm* the one with personal experience with Mick Myers! I'm the one he's serious about."

"Come off it, Julia—" Jessica began.

"Wait a minute, Jessica. This sounds even worse than I thought," Lila said. She turned to Julia. "You've been going out with Mick?"

"Well, sure," Julia said. "I mean, I didn't want to

broadcast it, because I know you both thought he liked you. But I guess it's time you knew the truth."

"What truth?" Jessica asked.

"That Mick likes me best," Julia said happily. "I'm sorry, Lila. But he said he was only going out with you because your uncle owns the place." She turned to smirk at Jessica. "And he called you a dumb blonde."

Jessica bristled.

"Julia," began Lila uncertainly. "I hate to tell you this, but he called you a fat blob."

Now it was Julia's turn to bristle. And she wanted to punch the superior smile right off of Jessica's face.

"I don't believe it!" Julia said, shaking her head. "Mick never said that about me."

"You should have heard the things he was saying behind my back when I was going out with him," Marcy said sympathetically.

"He called you a mother hen," Lila said helpfully.

Marcy laughed. "I guess I've been called worse. It sounds as if Anne is the only one who escaped it this time."

"Not exactly," Jessica said. "He told me Anne was so boring that he'd had livelier conversations with the electronic readouts on the Weather Channel."

"What an insensitive clod!" Marcy said.

"No, he's not!" Julia said loyally. "Not to the girl he's really in love with."

Marcy sighed. "When did you first go out with him, Julia?"

"We had lunch together Tuesday and Wednesday."

Lila laughed coldly. "He told me he had to give a windsurfing lesson to some tourists at lunchtime Wednesday."

"He told me he had to go to a meeting," said Jessica.

Julia smiled haughtily. "I guess he didn't want to hurt your feelings. He took me to this wonderful bistro that he said he was saving for someone special."

"With local paintings on the walls and a great view of the bay," Lila supplied. "He took me there today. He told me I was someone special."

Julia was confused. Lila had described the place perfectly. "You must have misunderstood his intentions," she said uncertainly. "And then, last night, Mick and I went for a romantic moonlight swim at this private lagoon. He told me to wear my sexiest bathing suit."

Jessica and Lila glanced at each other, and Julia narrowed her eyes. She was sure they were about to laugh. "He wouldn't have taken me to that lagoon if he wasn't serious about me," she insisted. "It was like a postcard. You should have seen it."

"I did," Jessica said dryly. "Mick and I watched the sunset there yesterday. That must have been right before he took you there."

"And right after he took me there," Lila said. "We went for a swim in the afternoon, off a rock that jutted out into the water—"

"With tropical plants all around," Julia finished. She was mortified. "I can't believe he would do this to me."

"Believe it," Marcy said.

The three younger girls turned to her.

"Mick did it to me last year over spring break," Marcy explained with a shrug. "And to three other staff members he was dating at the same time."

Julia wanted to cry. But she couldn't! She refused to let Jessica and Lila see how upset she was. Mick had lied to her. He had told her she was beautiful and voluptuous. He had pretended he cared about her. Now he was probably laughing to his friends about how he had put one over on Julia, the fat blob.

Her only consolation was that he had done the same thing to Jessica and Lila, despite their perfect hair and perfect bodies.

"Don't feel bad," Marcy told her. "It's not your fault. Every girl Mick's ever dated believed he was in love with her."

"He's even more of a creep than I thought!" Jessica exclaimed. "But he's not going to get away with it."

Marcy shrugged. "There's nothing you can do about it. He's been getting away with this stuff for years."

Jessica narrowed her beautiful blue eyes. "He's never tangled with Jessica Wakefield and Lila Fowler before."

Julia was interested, in spite of herself. "What are you going to do?"

"Operation Revenge," Jessica said. "We're going to make him look like a fool—in front of as many people as possible."

"We're still working out the details of our plan," Lila admitted. "But can we count on help from both of you?"

Julia looked carefully at Jessica and Lila. She still didn't trust any girl who was as gorgeous as they were. But when it came down to it, they were all girls. Sometimes, girls had to put aside their differences and work together against the real, true enemy—boys.

"Absolutely," Julia answered in a serious voice.

"I think you're being unrealistic," Marcy said. "But I guess I'm in too."

Jessica smiled. "Good. Here's the basic plan. We'll do it at the big talent show tomorrow night—"

Before she could continue, the bunkhouse door opened and Anne strolled in. She closed the door behind her and leaned against it, sighing dreamily.

"I just had another date with the best-looking boy in the world," she said. "His name is Mick Myers. I'm in love!"

"I don't want to see my mother hurt," Elizabeth said staunchly, "even if she is having an affair with your father."

"Aha!" Bruce yelled. "So you finally believe that they're having an affair!"

It was Friday morning, and they were sitting in a cool, enclosed veranda at the Patman mansion, overlooking the steamy gardens. Despite the fact that she was gorgeous, Bruce had never really liked Elizabeth Wakefield—in fact, he thought of her as one of the most uptight, sanctimonious kids at school.

Actually, he reminded himself, *there was that one time, early in the school year.* Elizabeth had amnesia and her defenses were down. Bruce had tried to take

164

advantage of her—what guy wouldn't? Unfortunately, she got her memory back just in time, ran right out of his house, and wrecked his plans for the evening.

Despite that incident, Bruce had never realized just how naive Elizabeth was. He couldn't believe that he still had to convince her that Alice Wakefield and Henry Patman were an item.

Elizabeth shook her head helplessly. "I don't know, Bruce. I have to admit that it really does look that way. The fact that they were married before, and hid it from us—"

"And the fact that they went to Chicago together—"

"Okay, okay. You're right. But the evidence is still circumstantial."

"Now you sound like your father—Ned Wakefield, hot-shot lawyer."

Elizabeth jumped up. "Don't you dare criticize my father! Isn't it bad enough that you're dragging my mother's name through the mud?"

"For Pete's sake, Liz, don't have a fit. Nobody's criticizing your precious father. Ned Wakefield is a pillar of the community, a gentleman and a scholar, a fine, upstanding—"

"Shut up, Bruce!"

For a minute, Bruce felt sorry for Elizabeth. The poor girl looked so confused and upset. Maybe he was being too hard on her.

Nah, he decided. Why should he cut her any slack? Elizabeth—the calm, reasonable Wakefield—had turned into a nervous wreck.

"Sit down, Liz," he ordered firmly. He was surprised when she obeyed him without protest. "Get a grip on yourself. This is too important for you to start acting like your wacko sister!"

"Darn you, Bruce!"

Bruce raised his eyebrows. It was the closest he'd ever heard Elizabeth Wakefield come to swearing. *She's actually kind of interesting when she's seething mad,* he realized, surprised.

"Is there anyone in my family that you haven't slandered yet?" Elizabeth asked. "What about my brother Steven? What about our golden lab? Surely there's something about Prince Albert that bugs you."

"He's a hairball," Bruce said. "And he has dog breath."

Elizabeth laughed in spite of herself.

"Okay," Bruce said. "Let's call a truce. It's the only way we're going to be able to accomplish anything."

"What do you mean?"

"You're supposed to be the smartest girl in the junior class. Do I have to spell out everything for you? My father and your mother are having a cheap, sordid affair. What are we going to do about it?"

"Even if it were true, what could we do about it? After all, it isn't really any of our business."

"Not any of our business? Are you insane? Of course it's our business. They're talking about breaking up our families. That will wreck our lives, too, Liz. We're not brother and sister, but we could be someday—whether we like it or not."

Elizabeth's blue-green eyes widened with fear. "So what are we going to do about it?"

"I don't know yet," Bruce said. "But we have to show them that we know about their secret marriage, and convince them that getting back together would be a big mistake. They'll deny it all if we can't prove that they were married and are seeing each other now. The photograph is a good start, but we need more proof before we confront them with the truth."

"I feel funny about trying to find evidence to use against my own mother. I'll help you investigate. But I'm not looking for proof that they're guilty. I'm looking for the truth!"

"Spare me the sanctimonious garbage, Liz—"

A uniformed butler appeared in the doorway. "Miss Wakefield's friends have arrived," he announced.

"Thanks," Elizabeth told him, with the first genuine smile Bruce had seen from her all morning. "Tell them I'll be right there."

Bruce shook his head. Only Elizabeth Wakefield would thank a servant for doing his job.

"I've got to go, Bruce. Olivia and Enid and I are going to lunch before the movie. It's an old Cary Grant film I've never seen before—*My Favorite Wife.*"

Elizabeth realized what she had just said, and her shoulders slumped. "Have you seen it, Bruce? Am I going to regret this?"

"Probably," Bruce said, smiling cruelly. *Someone as naive as Elizabeth deserves to be shaken up a little more.*

"I'm glad I could get away from the brats for lunch, Mick," Jessica said. "This bistro is fabulous. Those must be local paintings on the walls—right?"

"That's right," Mick said grandly. "Nothing but the

167

best for my golden goddess. This is one of my favorite places on the island to eat lunch. I usually come here for the view of the bay. But today I can't seem to take my eyes off you."

Jessica smiled fawningly. A day earlier, she would have been drowning in the liquid blue of his eyes. But there was no way he could draw her into those eyes today. Still, she couldn't help thinking, it was a shame that such a gorgeous hunk had turned out to be a two-timing jerk.

"Mick," she said, leaning forward so that the collar of her shirt fell open—just enough to be provocative. "Can you do me one itsy-bitsy little favor tonight?"

"Anything, my goddess," Mick said, his eyes on her top button.

"Tonight is that awful talent show I've been dreading all week. And that fiasco with Bobby's magic tricks yesterday has given me an idea. I'm going to do a magic act—but this time, I'm the magician."

"You've certainly cast a spell on me," Mick said.

Oh brother, Jessica thought ruefully. *Did I really fall for this stuff?* She took a deep breath. "I could really use your help with my magic act, Mick. Would you be my assistant?"

"Gee, Jess. Of course, I want to help you. But don't you think that could be uncomfortable for you—with that catty Lila Fowler there, too? I mean, you and I know how I really feel about Lila. But she doesn't know I'm only being nice to her because of her uncle. If she sees me helping with your act, it might make her angry with you. And I could get in trouble with Jimmo."

"I'm still so mad at Lila that I can hardly see straight," Jessica said. "I don't care if she hates me any more than she already does. As for Uncle Jimmo, I know how we can keep you in the clear. You can't get in trouble if I *force* you to help me with my act. So I'll reserve a seat for you in the first row. When I ask for a volunteer from the audience, you raise your hand and I'll pick you. Everybody—including Lila—will think you had nothing to do with it."

"You're incredible," Mick said, stroking the side of her face. "You're not only beautiful, but you're also brilliant—and persuasive. Do you always get exactly what you want?"

Jessica smiled, but her eyes were dead serious. "Absolutely."

Amy and Caroline stood in line in front of the Plaza Theatre after lunch on Friday.

"*My Favorite Wife,* starring Cary Grant," Caroline read aloud from the billboard. "Have you seen this before? Is it any good?"

"I haven't seen it," Amy replied. "But does it matter if it's good? This is the hottest day we've had yet. At least the theater is air-conditioned!"

"Cary Grant was pretty cute in yesterday's movie," Caroline said. "I hope he's as cute in this one."

Amy stared at the crowd milling around on the sidewalk outside the ticket window. "There are a lot of people here," she said. "Almost everyone from school who's in town this week!"

She waved at Elizabeth, Enid, and Olivia, standing in line about ten feet behind Amy and Caroline.

Enid and Olivia nodded, but Elizabeth didn't seem to notice Amy.

Caroline noticed. "Elizabeth Wakefield has been acting kind of spaced out the last couple days," she commented, pulling her red hair away from her sunburned face. "It's like she's preoccupied with something."

"You know Liz," Amy said with a shrug. "She's intent on this family-biography project. Plus, she's probably pining away over Todd being gone."

"Speaking of family biographies, how's your paper coming along?"

"Mr. Wakefield gave me some interesting information last night. I'm sure I can make up enough extra stuff to fill in the blanks. But I haven't actually started writing yet. There's no use destroying spring break with studying, until it's absolutely necessary."

"Spring break is already destroyed, between this heat and the fact that all the interesting people are out of town."

Amy laughed. "So what's the latest gossip? Is there any word on Bruce's parents?"

Caroline shook her head. "I'm drawing a blank on that one. Nobody seems to have even heard that Mr. Patman is having an affair, let alone the name of the other woman. I may have to give up on it until next week, when there are more people around to be observant for me. I can't be everywhere at once, you know."

The girls approached the ticket window, and Amy could see the movie poster displayed on the wall next to it. "From what I've heard about *My Favorite*

Wife," she explained, "Grant remarries because he thinks his first wife is dead. And then the first wife shows up, alive."

"That makes two movies in a row about people getting back together with their old loves," Caroline said. "How romantic! It's too bad real life isn't that exciting."

"You're right," Amy said. "Those things don't ever happen in real life."

"I thought we were supposed to play water sports!" six-year-old Heidi protested, as Jessica and Lila led their combined group of children to an out-of-the-way picnic area on Friday afternoon.

"There's been a change in plans," Lila explained. "We've decided to put you kids with Jessica's group to work on a special project."

Heidi wrinkled her nose. "But they're the nasty kids."

"We are not nasty!" Jessica's biggest boy protested. "And I'll bite anyone who says we are!"

"No, you won't bite anyone, Lorenzo," Jessica said firmly.

"But we don't want to play with wimpy kids," Karen complained.

"Nobody said anything about playing," Jessica told her. "We have serious business to discuss this afternoon."

Bartholomew politely tugged on the hem of Lila's shorts. "What kind of business?"

"We're going to play a little joke on someone," Lila said in a light, playful tone.

Jessica stared at each of her own little mutants in turn, her blue eyes narrowed. "How would you like to help us make somebody look really stupid in front of everyone?"

Gerry Pat grinned as he stared up at Jessica. "What do we get to do? Another magic show?"

"As a matter of fact, yes."

"You won't be onstage this time, kids," Lila said. "Children aren't allowed in this show, only counselors and staff."

Bobby crossed his arms jealously. "Then who's going to be the magician?"

"I am," Jessica said. "But I'm counting on you to teach me everything you know, Bobby. And I'll need to borrow your bag of tricks—though I've got a few tricks up my own sleeve, as well."

Lila grinned approvingly. "You always do, Jess."

Chapter 13

"I found a snake!" Heidi bragged in the Kiddie Kabana late Friday afternoon as Jessica and the kids put the finishing touches on that night's magic show.

Jessica watched as Lila's most adorable six-year-old thrust a wiggling snake in front of Bartholomew's face. The little boy yelped loudly.

Jessica examined the snake. "It's only rubber, Bart."

"I stole it from one of the big boys," Heidi explained with a proud smile. "Lorenzo showed me how."

"I did not!" Lorenzo screamed.

"You did too," said Heidi. "And I'll bite you if you say you didn't!"

Lorenzo's mouth dropped open, and he sat down without another word.

"You can't let a girl scare you, Bart!" Bobby yelled.

Bartholomew slapped him. "I was not scared!" he screamed.

"What's happened to them?" Anne asked, joining Jessica and the children. "Aren't those Lila's perfect little angels?"

Jessica felt a twinge of guilt. "They used to be," she said. "But after one afternoon with my little monsters, they seem—well, different!"

Angelic Heidi had become aggressive. Quiet Bartholomew had become loud. And even little Kayla—one of the "fraidy-cat girls" Bobby had criticized for crying—was sitting with Maria in the dirt at Jessica's feet. Both girls were calmly eating ants.

I am not going to worry about it, Jessica resolved. "After tonight, they're all their parents' responsibility, anyway," she said. "Operation Revenge is more important now."

"Here's the script," said the tall, dark-skinned girl. "You're about to become Jessica the Magnificent. But I'm going to be Anne the Unemployed if I don't get back to my kids. I left them with Charles. I'll see you tonight."

"Have Gerry Pat, Karen, and the other little girl and boy come back with more purple dye yet?" Jessica asked the children after Anne had gone.

"Nope," Suzy said. "It's not fair! They get to steal dye from the big kids' art room, and I have to stay in the Kiddie Banana with the rest of the wimpy kids."

"We are not wimpy kids!" Bartholomew screamed. "You're nasty kids!" He stuck his tongue out at Suzy—and then curled it upward to touch the tip of his nose.

"How did you learn to do that?" Suzy asked, impressed enough to ignore the insult. "My tongue's too little."

"Karen showed me how," Bartholomew said proudly. "I can't wait to show Lila. I bet she'll like me even better!"

"But I'm Lila's favorite!" Heidi insisted.

"No, you're not! I am!" Bart screamed.

"When is Lila coming back?" Kayla asked.

"She had to pick up some things for the show tonight," Jessica said. "You'll see her at dinner."

"We're here!" Gerry Pat cried, running up to Jessica. Karen and two of Lila's charges followed him.

"We brought lots of purple dye," Karen said. "What are you going to use it for?"

"Sorry. That's a secret," Jessica said.

Maria looked up hopefully. "Will you make my eyes purple?"

"No, but somebody else is going to be seeing red!"

Enid shielded her eyes from the white-hot gleam of late-afternoon sunshine off the surface of Secca Lake. She had just come from Friday's movie with Elizabeth and Olivia. The three girls were now sitting in the grass at the popular recreation area. "I guess this wasn't such a good idea," Enid said. "I thought maybe it would be a little cooler here than in town."

"It probably is a little cooler here," Olivia said. "Unfortunately, that means it's one hundred and eight degrees instead of one hundred and ten."

Enid looked curiously at Elizabeth. "So what's the verdict on today's movie?" Enid asked. "Should Cary Grant have stayed with his second wife, or was he right to have gone back to Irene Dunne, after he found out she was still alive?"

Elizabeth threw up her hands. "I don't know anymore," she said. "And it's too hot to think."

Enid and Olivia exchanged a concerned glance. For some reason, Elizabeth had let Bruce's idiotic stories ruin her whole week. Surely Elizabeth knew better than to believe his lies.

"How is your research going?" Enid asked.

Elizabeth gave her a tired smile. "I've found a few stories about Mom's life that I can use in my paper. My father told me about the first time they met—"

Enid shook her head. "You know that's not what I mean."

"I know," Elizabeth said, scratching a mosquito bite on her leg. "You're talking about the research to prove that my mother isn't having an affair with Bruce's father. Well, there isn't much to say about it."

"You still haven't found anything to prove she's innocent?" Olivia asked.

"No," Elizabeth said miserably.

"So stop looking," Enid told her. "Forget about Bruce. You know your mother has never loved anyone but your father. Your whole family knows it. Isn't that enough?"

Elizabeth shook her head. "No," she whispered. "It isn't."

Friday night's talent show was held in an indoor auditorium, not far from the Kiddie Korral. *It's not exactly Broadway,* Jessica thought. But the place had a real stage, with a curtain and spotlights. Of course, that was no surprise to Jessica. Her pint-sized spies had checked out the setup ahead of time. Mick's punishment would have more of an impact on him if the whole act seemed professional. When he decided to mess with Jessica and Lila, Mick wasn't taking on a couple of amateurs. In another two hours, he would understand that.

Now Jessica peered out at the audience from behind the curtain. Julia was onstage, singing her rendition of "Wilkommen," as the opening act in tonight's show. Jessica's magic act would be the last performance of the evening.

"Is everything in place?" Lila whispered, touching Jessica on the shoulder.

"You look terrific!" Jessica whispered back. "Where did you get the Sugar Plum Fairy dress?"

"From Renata's formalwear store. You're never going to believe this, but Mick started dating *her* this week, too! After I told her the truth about him, Renata was happy to let me borrow the dress for free. And look at my trick gloves. Your little brat, Bobby, gave me the idea. Renata let me have a pair of these old, elbow-length formal gloves, and I cut a few slits in them. I can't exactly hide a rubber chicken in there, but they'll do for a few little things. And all these filmy layers in my skirt and shawl will conceal other important items."

Jessica laughed, covering her mouth with her hand. "I just can't wait to see the look on Mick's face when you show up onstage during my act. He'll know he's been caught, but he won't be able to do a single thing about it!"

"Anne said she'd try to take some photos," Lila

promised, a vindictive gleam in her eye. "You know, to preserve those tender moments. But I forgot to tell you—Renata also found some things for you to wear!"

Lila held out a black tuxedo jacket, a sparkling silver cummerbund, and a red-lined cape. "These will be fabulous with your leather miniskirt, Jessica. And there's a top hat, too. You'll love the jacket, Jess. It's not just a tuxedo jacket—it's really from a magician's suit. The sleeves are big enough for all the junk you wanted to cram up there—and they even have special pockets."

Jessica grinned. "Perfect. And that cape sure beats Bobby's plastic rain poncho."

Lila laughed. "I made sure to bump into Mick before the show started," she said.

"How is the guest of honor? He doesn't suspect anything, does he?"

"Not a thing. I pretended to be crazy about him, of course, and he lapped it up, like he always did. It made my skin crawl to do it, but I had to keep up the illusion that everything's the same as it was yesterday."

"Illusion is right," Jessica whispered. "Tonight, Jessica the Magnificent will teach Mick the Maggot all about illusions."

"It's all an illusion, man," Bruce said, leaning back on the bed in his large bedroom at the Patman estate. It was Friday night, and Bruce's cousin Roger had just come into his room for one of those heart-to-heart brotherly chats that Bruce usually hated so much.

Roger looked perplexed. "What's an illusion, Bruce?"

"Life, love, family, being in control. All of it."

"Bruce, have you been drinking?"

Bruce scowled. "No, I haven't been drinking. I'm perfectly sober and perfectly serious!"

Roger would not have been Bruce's first choice for talking out his new philosophy with, but Roger had one enormous asset—he was there. Unlike most of Bruce's real friends, Roger hadn't gone out of town with his parents. *Of course, Roger has no parents,* Bruce reminded himself.

Bruce remembered feeling so superior to Roger. *I thought I had this perfect little family, while Roger had none,* he said to himself. *Then, last weekend, I thought my perfect family was losing control, tearing itself apart. But it wasn't, because it was never perfect to begin with.*

His parents hadn't screwed up their marriage. It had been flawed from the start. Flawed by a secret, early marriage to a pretty blonde named Alice.

Of course, in a lot of ways, Bruce still felt superior to Roger. He was more handsome, more popular, and more talented. Sure, Roger had money now. But Roger couldn't inherit real style—not the kind of style Bruce had been born with.

Or is that an illusion too?

"Everything you count on, your whole life long, is just so much hot air," Bruce said. "It seems solid, but one day, you discover that it's not. It's an illusion."

"Does this have anything to do with your parents' marriage?" Roger asked tentatively.

"You know, Roger, sometimes you are really dense!"

179

"Sorry, man. I'm only trying to help."

Bruce jumped up from the bed and faced Roger angrily. "Well, don't help!" he yelled, stifling an urge to punch his cousin in the face. "There's nothing you can do anyway. How could Dad lie to us all? How could he pretend for so many years?"

He threw himself back on the bed and stared at the ceiling. "I'm not going to take this lying down."

"Bruce, anything that may have happened is between your parents. There's nothing you can do about it."

Bruce shook his head. Roger sounded just like Elizabeth.

"I refuse to believe I'm completely powerless," he said. "What I need is information. It's one of the first tenets of warfare—or big business," Bruce added, still staring at the ceiling. "Know your enemy."

"What do you mean?"

"It's none of your business," Bruce said with a sneer.

He was glad when Roger shrugged his shoulders and left the room. He had no intention of telling Roger about Elizabeth's discovery. Having to tiptoe around Elizabeth was bad enough. Bruce refused to humor two weak-willed bleeding hearts who didn't understand the need for decisive action in a situation like this.

At least being stuck with Elizabeth had some rewards. Elizabeth was attractive.

Besides, Bruce found the whole situation incredibly embarrassing. Within reason, it was all right for a respected businessman to have a sordid past. But only if he kept it hidden. Anything else was down-right tacky. So was a college-age marriage to a flower-child artist from the wrong side of the tracks.

Bruce didn't want anyone else to know about his father's past marriage and current affair—for as long as possible. Of course, when his parents and the Wakefields got divorces so that Henry could marry Alice, the awful truth would come tumbling out. And Bruce's reputation would be ruined forever.

Unless he and Elizabeth could find some way to stop the inevitable.

"Information," he said again, this time to the empty room. "We need to know more about what happened twenty-five years ago."

"For our final performance of the evening, Kiddie Paradise presents a very special act," Trixie intoned from a backstage microphone Friday night, cheer-fully reading aloud from the script Jessica had given her.

"Direct from Southern California, it's that Mistress of Magic, that Goddess of Enchantment—Jessica the Magnificent!"

Jessica was grateful for Anne's help on the script. Now, she knew, Anne was backstage, ready to help with any necessary chores. And Marcy and Julia were perched in the crawl space beneath the stage, waiting for their own part in tonight's show.

A spotlight poured over Jessica's body, and she drank it in. Jessica had felt this same rush of adrenalin in every school play she'd ever done—not to mention the television soap opera she and Elizabeth had guest-starred on earlier that year. Once again, Jessica realized how much she loved being the star. And tonight was even better. The spotlight was sweet, but revenge was even sweeter.

"First, I'll need a volunteer from the audience," Jessica announced.

She deftly pulled a bouquet of colorful paper flowers from thin air—well, they were actually from her sleeve, but nobody else could see that. She tossed the bouquet into the audience, aiming for Mick in the front row. He caught it and pretended to be embarrassed when the spotlight bathed him in its yellow glow. Jessica had found a "volunteer."

She started with a few of Bobby's simple card tricks. Then she was ready to call in the big guns.

"For this next trick, I'm going to need a little extra help from a colleague in the magic profession," Jessica explained. "May I present my good friend, Fowler the Fantastic!"

Mick's blue eyes widened in horror when Lila stepped out from behind the curtain and made a deep curtsy. Jessica noticed the flare of a flashbulb and smiled. Anne was making good on her promise to capture Mick's expressions on film.

Lila held out her hand to Mick. "May I have your watch, please, sir?"

Mick unbuckled his expensive wristwatch and handed it, uncertainly, to Lila.

"Pay close attention, ladies and gentlemen," Lila intoned, "to this perfectly normal wristwatch."

She carefully wrapped the watch in a piece of fabric—actually, the remains of Jessica's purple-stained shirt—and handed the bundle to Jessica.

"Abracadabra!" Jessica said importantly. "The hand is quicker than the eye."

If Jessica had been performing the trick in the usual way, the watch wouldn't have been there at all. She already would have slipped it out of the fabric bundle and into her pocket, without anyone seeing. Then she would smash the bundle with a hammer until everyone was convinced that the watch was shattered into a million fragments. At the end, Jessica would slip the watch back into the piece of fabric. When she unwrapped the bundle, the watch would be intact.

But Jessica had worked out her own variation on the trick. And for her version, Mick's watch would still be in the bundle when she pummeled it with the hammer.

"Have you ever looked for a way to kill time?" Jessica asked the audience. She picked up the hammer and pounded it several times against the purplish bundle. Only the three people onstage could hear the crunch of breaking glass.

Mick's face fell.

"I guess you've all heard the old saying about how time flies," Jessica said to the audience in a conversational tone. Then she unfolded the purple bundle, slowly, while holding it up so the audience could see.

The watch was gone.

The shattered pieces of Mick's watch were in Jessica's trick sleeve. To her audience, of course, the watch seemed to have disappeared. Everyone clapped enthusiastically.

Jessica saw that Mick knew exactly what was happening. He knew that Jessica and Lila had compared stories and discovered the truth about him. He knew they were now getting their revenge. And he knew that his watch looked like breakfast cereal. What he didn't know was how to get offstage and out of the line of fire. He couldn't save himself without being embarrassed. He was at Jessica's mercy. "Okay, girls," he whispered. "You've had your fun."

"Mick, darling," Jessica whispered back, "you ain't seen nothing yet."

She pulled a quarter out of Mick's left ear, and another one from under his long, silky hair.

"What else do you think is in there?" she asked the audience. The next time Jessica reached behind Mick's ear, she meant business. She held a pair of scissors concealed in her hand. Mick stiffened when he heard the sickening snip of the shears as they cut through his beautiful blond hair. Jessica pulled a red rose out of Mick's hair, smiling broadly at the audience. A lock of Mick's golden hair fell in a clump at her feet.

Mick looked positively green—and it wasn't from the spotlights. "You wouldn't," he whispered to Jessica, a pleading look in his eyes.

"Too late," Jessica mouthed at him. "I already did."

"Look at the big man on the beach now," Lila whispered triumphantly. She was surprised at how easy it had been to intimidate Mick. He wasn't even resisting. In fact, the windsurfer looked as if he was about to hyperventilate.

Now it was Lila's turn to have some fun. Jessica passed her the scissors, unseen, and Lila pulled a succession of silver dollars out of Mick's head, cutting off another lock of golden hair with each coin.

From the front, Mick's head still looked perfectly normal. But Lila could barely restrain her laughter when she saw the back of his head. She and Jessica had taken care to clip his hair in uneven, ragged strokes.

Lila reached behind Mick's head one last time, and then pulled out her hand in a dramatic gesture.

"How in the world did these get in there?" she asked into the microphone, deadpan.

The audience broke into hysterical laughter. Lila was holding up a pair of panty hose.

Mick's face was as red as the lining in Jessica's cape.

"For the grand finale," Lila announced when the audience quieted down, "Jessica the Magnificent will amaze and delight you, by making our volunteer from the audience disappear!"

The audience applauded. Backstage, Anne began a drumroll. The lights dimmed until only the violet spotlight glowed.

"First, the magic pixie dust!" Jessica intoned, sprinkling purple powder on Mick's head.

Then Lila and Jessica held up a sheet, screening Mick from the audience. Behind the sheet, an invisible trapdoor in the stage floor opened. Julia popped up through it, grabbed Mick, and led him into the crawl space beneath the stage.

Mick seemed grateful to follow her down.

"Mick looked like he wanted to sink into the floor," Lila whispered to Jessica behind the sheet. "His wish has come true."

"Abracadabra!" Jessica said loudly. When the sheet fell, Mick had vanished without a trace.

Julia couldn't believe this was working so well. She almost felt sorry for Mick. But not quite.

The back of his head looked as if someone had cut his hair with a hedge clipper. Jessica and Lila had proven themselves to be master schemers, as well as master performers. Now it was Julia and Marcy's turn.

At first, they played it straight, as if this were part of a legitimate magic trick.

"This way, Mick," Julia said, ushering him down the short flight of steps that led to the area beneath the stage. She kept a firm grasp on his left arm. Marcy was hanging on to his right. Mick seemed too dazed to do more than follow along.

This was turning out to be much easier than Julia had expected. *Who would have thought Mick would turn into such a simpering little wimp as soon as a few girls held him accountable for the rotten way he'd treated them?* she thought.

"What happens now?" Mick asked. "Why is it so dark?"

"Don't worry, the show's almost over," Marcy assured him. Julia handed Mick a wet towel.

"What's this for?" he asked.

"To wipe out that purple pixie dust Jessica sprinkled you with," Marcy explained. "Make sure the towel's sopping wet, and rub hard with it. That powder can be hard to get out."

"Do we have time?" Mick asked. "Don't I need to reappear onstage?"

"You've got a few minutes," Julia assured him as he began rubbing his ragged hair with the wet towel. "This is when Jessica goes into a spiel about following you into the spirit world. You know how melodramatic she can get."

A flashing light was the girls' cue to bring Mick back onstage. The weird, violet spotlight made Julia feel disoriented as she deposited Mick back on his stool, behind the sheet that Lila and Jessica were holding up again.

"Abracadabra!" Jessica called. "Return from the land of darkness! Jessica the Magnificent has spoken."

Elizabeth was lying listlessly across her bed Friday night, thinking about *My Favorite Wife,* when the phone rang.

Amy's voice greeted her. "Hi, Liz," Amy said. "I saw you at the movie today, but I don't think you noticed me."

"Oh, were you there too?"

"I wanted to talk to you about our English papers."

Elizabeth wanted to forget all about her English paper. Initially, her problem with writing it was that her mother didn't have anything dramatic in her past. Now her mother's past seemed *too* dramatic. Elizabeth didn't want to write about Alice's first marriage.

But her paper would be deadly dull without it. Except for the story about Ned Wakefield pulling Alice out of the ocean, Elizabeth hadn't learned anything else of interest. But she knew she had to make a decision about the biography soon.

Elizabeth tried to focus her thoughts. Thinking about a school project had to be better than moping around and worrying about a movie.

"Elizabeth? Are you still there? How is your research going? Have you discovered anything else about your family that may be useful in your paper? Even something from as far back as, say, Jessamyn's time could turn out to be important. You never know when something that occurred in a past generation might give you a new insight into a more recent event."

Now Amy sounds like she's playing Project Youth counselor, Elizabeth thought. But, she admitted, Amy was making sense.

"Have you found out anything new about Jessamyn?" Amy asked.

Elizabeth was puzzled. Amy seemed almost fixated on the Wakefields' ancestors. *She really ought to be spending more time on her own great-great-grandmother,* Elizabeth thought, *and less time on Jessamyn.*

But Amy's fixation gave Elizabeth an idea for her own paper.

"Maybe I do have something to report," Elizabeth said. She was beginning to feel interested, in spite of herself. "You're absolutely right, Amy. Events from a past generation can influence the present."

"Huh?"

"You've just given me an idea. I've been agonizing over Mom's lack of an exciting past. But she *does* have an exciting past—going back into the last century! Maybe I can incorporate some of the stories of the women who were her ancestors into my mother's story. I can show how the life of somebody like Jessamyn affected Mom's life. I can trace similar characteristics through several generations."

For some reason, Amy seemed dismayed. "Do you mean that you would tell in your paper about how Jessamyn was a bareback rider in the circus?"

"That's right," Elizabeth said. "And about her twin daughters, and about her sister Elisabeth, and about my grandmother. . . . You know, I think I'm really onto something."

"I'm not sure that's a good idea," Amy said quickly. "I mean, it's supposed to be a biography. Shouldn't you keep the focus on your mother?"

"You're right," Elizabeth said. "And I will. I'll only use the stories of the other women to show their relationships to my mother's life. Amy, you're a genius!"

The audience applauded as Mick "reappeared." He sat onstage, blinking in the weird, purple light. When the spotlight turned white, the audience erupted into wild laughter. *Mick's hair was bright purple!*

Jessica's magic pixie dust was powdered dye—the same kind that Bobby, Gerry Pat, and Lorenzo had used on Maria's curls a few days earlier.

When the curtain dropped, Jessica and Lila were both laughing hysterically. Mick stared from one girl to the other, looking more worried by the moment.

Then he jumped up and ran backstage, to a dressing room with a mirror.

Jessica threw her arms around Lila.

"We schemed against each other all week," she said, "but we still managed to work together to come up with a brilliant plan and make it a success. I think that says a lot about our relationship."

Lila grabbed the top hat from Jessica's head and placed it on her own. "What it says is that we were *meant* to be best friends."

"You'll never believe the conversation I just had with Elizabeth Wakefield," Amy wailed into her bedroom phone.

"What happened?" Caroline asked. "Did you learn any good dirt on anyone?"

"Do you ever let it rest, Caroline? This isn't about gossip. This is about my life! And it's ruined! Elizabeth decided to incorporate Jessamyn's story into her biography of her mother. And *I* gave her the idea!"

"That wasn't very smart."

"I didn't do it on purpose, dummy. The point is, I can't write about Jessamyn if Elizabeth's going to mention her in her own paper. Mr. Collins would never believe that both of us have great-great-grandmothers who ran away from home at sixteen to become bareback riders in the circus!"

"Maybe you can let him think she was really your relative, and Elizabeth borrowed her."

"Are you kidding? Elizabeth Wakefield, superstudent? Collins thinks she's perfect. He'd never believe it."

"So what are you going to do?"

"Something really desperate," Amy said in a miserable voice. "But I have no choice. I'm going to write about my own mother."

"Where are those two witches?" Mick yelled from the dressing room backstage, after the final curtain calls.

Onstage, behind the closed curtains, Lila smiled at Jessica. She thought that Jessica looked a little nervous.

"What do you think he'll do to us?" Jessica asked.

Lila shrugged. "What can he do? He has purple hair, and it's butchered in back. And every girl he's duped is loving every minute of it."

"This will go down in Club Paradise legend!" Marcy said as she joined them onstage. "As soon as the grapevine begins working, everyone will know the full story behind tonight's show. It'll be years before Mick will be able to get a date at this resort!"

Suddenly, Mick himself appeared in the wings. He looked mad enough to breathe fire. "This stuff doesn't come out of my hair!" he screamed.

"It will come out eventually," Lila assured him. "What did you say, Jess? A month or so?"

"Probably a couple months, in Mick's case," Jessica explained. "We used a more concentrated form than the boys put on Maria's hair."

Mick pointed at Jessica and Lila. "You two witches are the masterminds behind this. Don't deny it!"

"Why would we want to deny it?" Jessica asked.

"Lila and I believe in giving credit where credit is due."

"You're going to be sorry for this!" Mick yelled. He lunged toward them, and then stopped dead. In a circle around Jessica and Lila, a dozen kindergarten-age children had suddenly materialized. Several of them were holding sticks.

"If you hurt our counselors, I'll bite you!" Lorenzo warned.

"I see that the wicked witches have their gang of trained munchkin thugs," Mick said.

Jessica laughed. "It looks like they're enough to defeat you, Mick."

"I'll get you both for this!" He hurled the empty threat backward at Jessica and Lila as he stormed off the stage.

"Will he come back?" Suzy asked.

"No," Marcy said. "Mick's a coward at heart. I don't think Jessica and Lila have to worry about him anymore." She turned to Jessica and Lila. "You did it, girls. You whipped him!"

Jessica stooped down to talk to the HLKs. "We didn't do it alone. You kids were terrific!"

"We scared him good!" Bartholomew bragged.

Lorenzo grinned broadly. "It was my idea!"

"You're in for it now, Jess," Lila warned as they stepped out of the auditorium after the show. "The rest of your HLKs' parents were all dying to meet you backstage." She grinned. "The only ones you haven't seen are Maria's parents!"

Jessica groaned. "Don't remind me. How do you

192

explain to a mother that her five-year-old's hair will be bright purple for the next month?"

"I'm sure you'll think of something."

Julia caught up with them in the building's entrance, breathless. "Hi, Lila," she said. She looked uncertainly at Jessica. "Hi, Jessica."

Jessica knew Julia didn't like her any better than she liked Julia. But they had managed to put aside their differences and work together that day—for the sake of Operation Revenge.

"Jessica, I—"

"It's all right, Julia," Jessica told her. "Let's not get mushy. But I appreciated your help today."

Julia smiled, obviously relieved. "Thanks, Jessica. And I really admire you—" she nodded at Lila, "both of you—for standing up to a jerk like Mick. I would never have had the guts to do something like that myself."

"Thank you," Jessica said. She hesitated a moment. "Lila and I are going to the Kiddie Banana for a late-night lemonade. Do you want to join us?"

"I'd love to—except that I, uh, sort of have a date."

"With who?" Jessica asked, more curious than she wanted to admit.

Julia blushed. "With Charles."

"Good for you," Lila said. "I thought you liked him."

"To tell you the truth, I'm still not sure if I do," Julia said. "But I can't leave Club Paradise with only Mick to show for my efforts, can I? And Charles is awfully nice."

Jessica rolled her eyes. "Well, I can't say that he's

193

my type, but you're welcome to him."

"I don't need your permission!" Julia snapped. Then she giggled. "Sorry. You know, Charles said you impressed him in the show tonight, Jessica."

Jessica laughed. "So what else is new?"

"He's decided that you're way out of his league. He said you were too devious for him!"

"Which leaves the field open for you," Jessica concluded. "Sweet, retiring, nondevious, unmanipulative Julia. You've got him snowed."

Julia winked. "Exactly."

"Looks like it's just you and me, kid," Jessica quipped to Lila after Julia ran off.

"I don't know about that," Lila said, pretending to be very serious as she pushed open the door to the outside. "I should be mad at you. You're a bad influence. You corrupted my perfect little children, Wakefield—"

"So you're Jessica Wakefield!" said a tall, curly-haired woman who was waiting outside. "Of course, I recognize you from the show. Jessica, I must talk to you right away. I'm Maria's mother."

Jessica hesitated for only a fraction of a second.

"I'm so sorry, ma'am," she said politely. "But you want my twin sister. My name is Elizabeth Wakefield!"

The headlights from a passing car made geometric patterns on the walls of Elizabeth's room. Then the room was dark again. Elizabeth lay in bed, staring up at the ceiling.

For a while, she had been able to distract herself

194

by mentally outlining her English paper—concentrating, for now, only on the parts of her mother's life that she wanted to face. But now she was thinking about *My Favorite Wife,* for the twentieth time that day. Irene Dunne had come to reclaim her husband Cary Grant, but ran into a minor detail—he was remarried. It was just like Henry Patman, rekindling an old love affair with his former wife, now Alice Wakefield. . . .

"Why do I do this to myself?" Elizabeth asked.

She couldn't help thinking about the other movies she had seen that week. They all seemed to be about people going back to their first loves. In fact, the only movie character who didn't go back was Ingrid Bergman in *Casablanca.* And Elizabeth herself had argued that Bergman should have reunited with Bogart. They were *meant* to be together.

What if Elizabeth's mother was *meant* to be with Bruce's father? Maybe Alice's marriage to Ned Wakefield was just a meaningless interlude, a mistake in judgment. What then?

Elizabeth's head was spinning. Bruce's parents would go ahead with their divorce. Elizabeth's parents would split up, too. The next step would be for Alice Wakefield to marry Henry Patman. Elizabeth flopped over onto her stomach, as if hiding her head in her pillow could shut out the pictures that were crowding into her mind. But she could see her future much too clearly.

There would be a Patman wedding—huge, expensive, and stuffy—on the manicured grounds of the Patman mansion, among sculpted boxwood and overdressed people who looked down their noses at the middle-class Wakefields. Elizabeth and Jessica would have to wear something pink and frilly—and sticky in the sweltering heat, which showed no signs of letting up. Alice Wakefield would become Alice Patman. And Elizabeth and Jessica would move up the hill with her to the Patman residence, where they would be Bruce's stepsisters.

Elizabeth began to cry into her pillow—at first weeping quietly and then breaking into gut-wrenching sobs. Her family was ruined. Her life would never be the same.

Will Alice Wakefield become the next Mrs. Henry Patman? Find out in Sweet Valley High #102, **ALMOST MARRIED.**

*Starting in February 1994, look for books in
THE WILD ROSE INN series.*

*Each captivating novel is part of an unfolding
American family saga featuring generations
of young MacKenzie women, all growing up
at . . .*

Here's a preview of the first book,

BRIDIE OF THE WILD ROSE INN, 1695:

At the afternoon worship service, Bridie shared a smile with the girl that she'd seen that morning. And as the service ended, they found themselves walking out together with the others.

"You're Bridget MacKenzie, are you not?" the girl asked in a low voice. She was tall and willowy, with wheat-colored hair. "I'm called Sarah Furness."

"Let us be friends, Sarah," Bridie whispered. "I would like that."

"My family lives only across from yours," Sarah said. "Come find me when you can."

Then Sarah was gone, walking with a bowed head behind her mother and older sisters away from the meeting house. Bridie smiled. She'd indeed go looking for her new friend when she could. But for the moment there was business again at the MacKenzie ordinary, and she hurried home with her family, thinking sadly of her friend Kit, whom she'd left behind in Scotland.

The following morning Bridie set herself to see if the rose cuttings so hard cared for would take. Already she had taken notice of the wild roses that grew where the narrow, muddy streets dwindled into footpaths. She took a pick and dug one out and carried it back to the ordinary.

"What are you after?" her brother asked, seeing her attack the stony garden soil in the side yard with the pick.

"I'm grafting the slips I brought with me," she explained. "Johnny, fetch me a knife, do."

His green eyes met hers curiously, and then he shouldered open the door. In a moment he was back, holding out a knife in his hand. He squatted near her in the dirt, watching her careful incisions in the bark.

"We'll soon see if these will take," Bridie

told him, tying the grafts into place with thin strips of leather. Her fingers worked deftly with the wet twigs, and she felt the sun press warm on her back. She looked around and saw how firmly rooted the ordinary was to its rocky bed. Massachusetts was a place where all things could thrive. There was robust defiance wherever Bridie looked, and she valued the beauty it made of itself. She smiled and touched the grafts gently.

"Will they grow new on this plant?" John asked in wonderment. " 'Tis a marvelous thing to take dead sticks and make them live again."

"But they're not dead sticks," Bridie said. "The life's asleep down inside them, waiting to spring forth—like all there is around us here."

She pointed to the small new shoots of grass and plants that poked through the soil, and at a dauber wasp that crawled dazedly onto a sunny rock, opening its wings to warm itself in the pale sunlight. John looked at them and smiled up at her, his round face bright in the sun.

"Our grandfather knew all the care of

roses and other plants," Bridie continued. "He taught me a muckle of lore. He was a goodly man, Johnny, and I miss him very much."

John poked into the wet earth with a stick. "Miss you Scotland too?"

"Ah . . ." Bridie bowed her head, thinking of the home she had left, of Father Dougal and his homely, earnest face, of Kit's sharp laughter when Bridie sang off-key to tease her, of the smell of peat fires and the rumble of cartwheels leaving, leaving . . .

"I do," she said with a sigh.

"But are you not happy to be with us here?"

"Certainly I am," Bridie said. She gave him a swift kiss on the top of his head. "I wouldn't ever want to leave you, but it was my home, you know. I must bump into a good many things here until I find how I fit."

John gave her a puzzled grin, seemed ready to say something, and then shook his head. "What else do you know of plants?" he asked.

Bridie eased her back. "When I was your

age, I knew a great deal already. I know the plants back home, and I'm hoping that many are the same here. But already I have seen scores of new plants. They grow from every cranny and patch of earth. I will go out later and see which ones I know."

"Do not stray too far," her mother said, overhearing Bridie from the hallway. "The Indians are always hard by."

"But didn't you say that the Naumkeag were peaceable?" Bridie asked.

Her mother hugged her arms about herself and squinted at the sky. "They have been. But do not stray too far," she repeated, and she went back indoors with John following behind her.

Bridie was suddenly afire to be off alone, away from the new rules and strangeness of it all, away from the need to be always learning her way. She hastily wiped her hands on her apron and swept up her basket and cloak from beside the doorstep. Then, before anyone could tell her she was overstepping another line, she ran from the ordinary and out toward the rocky shore. She soon put the small town behind her. She'd search for plants, and then come back and find Sarah Furness.

The breeze whipped her heavy skirts around her legs as she tramped up through the long, tawny tussocks of grass and stepped around lichenous boulders. Always to her right was the rising, heaving mass of the ocean, glittering and vast. She scrambled up onto a rocky outcropping and stood looking out at the sea, holding her balance hard as the wind buffeted her. It was a magnificent prospect full of light. Sails she could see out on the water, and then the rolling slow arc of a whale's back as it crested far out and sounded the depths. Bridie felt an awe take hold of her, and she held out her arms to embrace the great ocean.

Then a sudden gust snatched the basket from her hand and tumbled it to the grass. Bridie jumped down to chase it and felt with dismay that her hair was coming loose from its pins. For a moment she stopped to catch the loose strands, but the basket gusted away again, and Bridie gave chase, laughing with frustration and the contrariness of the wind.

"What an unchancy wind." She gasped, swooping down on the basket before it could blow out of her reach again. She plumped down on the grass in a cuplike hollow, tucked one foot through the handle of the basket, and then addressed herself to her hair.

"Now, you'll stay," she ordered it, her eyes gleaming and her cheeks rosy with the wind. She coiled her hair on her head, feeling for the pins that never seemed to hold for long.

Then she stilled her hands, aware that she was not alone. Slowly she raised her eyes. A young man was standing at the rim of her grassy bowl, looking down at her in amazement. Bridie stared back at him, wondering what made him look so strangely at her. And then her hair tumbled down onto her shoulders again. Bridie giggled. She could not help it with the wild mood that was on her.

"What are you?" the young man said hoarsely, staring at her as though she were a spirit. His fine features were pulled awry by uncertainty, and his blue eyes were wide with dismay.

Bridie's brows arched. "I am a MacKenzie, is what I am, Will of God Handy."

He looked even more alarmed. "You know my name."

"And you ought to know mine and who I am, for you've seen me with my mother as I've seen you with yours," Bridie retorted, amused by his dazed manner. She wrestled again with her wild, willful hair and finally subdued it. She grasped the basket and stood up.

Will drew himself upright. "I am just returned from Salem," he said in a steady voice. "What do you here?"

"Learning this new land," she replied. "'Tis many ways alike to Scotland—these rocks and hills, this sweeping wind. But also unlike."

"How?" He looked around as though the notion of learning the land was new to him.

Bridie tipped her face to the sky. "This light. This ocean here," she said, opening her arms wide again. "'Tis very grand."

"'Tis dangerous and full of evil," Will said stiffly. He drew a shaky breath, and then his brow cleared, and Bridie saw he was a handsome fellow when the look of solemnity left him. "What do you gather?"

"I search for herbs that might heal," Bridie told him, wishing for an instant that her hair might come down again to rattle him.

His frown returned. "If it be God's will that a man sicken, none should hinder it."

"What a hard thing to say!" Bridie gasped. "It surely is not God's will that we suffer without need. I know physics and simples that might cure an aching head or strengthen the blood and make the body well." She looked at him hard. "The better to do God's work. 'Tis nowhere ordained that we should not help the sick."

Will shook his head stubbornly. "God has His plan and should not be hampered."

"God's plan includes the plants he put here for our use," Bridie insisted, pointing to the growing green all around.

"Nay."

"Och," Bridie gasped and brought her hand down hard by her side. Through the cloth of her skirt, she felt something sharp. Curious, she reached into her pocket and drew out the crooked nail she had picked up on the ship.

"Why do you carry such a talisman?" Will asked suspiciously.

"I don't carry it," she replied. "Not by design. Nor is it a talisman but a simple nail. I only picked it up for thrift."

Will looked affronted. "A crooked nail may not be so simple."

"I believe the fairies have been at you," Bridie said, laughing. She tossed the nail away only to shock and confound him more. "You're all mizzled in the head."

He flushed angrily, which tickled Bridie further. She knew she should cease her taunting, but she could not. She also knew that he could walk away from her but did not, and it brought color to her cheeks.

"And perhaps I'm the fairy that mizzled you," she went on, her eyes dancing. "Mayhap I've been sent by old Hornie himself to tempt you, as well."

"I know you jest, Mistress MacKenzie," Will said sternly. "But it is an evil thing to do."

Bridie laughed again. "Don't be so certain I do jest, for I may have powers you cannot reckon. The famousest seer of Scotland was a MacKenzie, you know, the Seer of Brahan from the Isle of Lewis. He could see the future through a hole in a little stone."

As Will looked on, dumbfounded, Bridie picked up a small rock and held it up. "They say he blint his eye by staring through the stone." She raised it to her eye.

"Don't!" Will exclaimed, and then flushed in embarrassment when she laughed.

Bridie had not enjoyed herself so much since she left Scotland. The effect she had on Will Handy delighted her, and she cast about for some other means to bring that look to his face. Then she began to sing.

"O, rattlin' roarin' Willie, he held to the fair,
An' for to sell his fiddle, and buy some other ware
But partin' wi' his fiddle, the salt tear blint his e'e
And rattlin' roarin' Willie, ye're welcome home to me!"

Bridie tucked her basket under her arm, sent a smile to the shocked Will, and walked away.

"What a ramping fool," she said, chuckling.

But she thought she'd like to see him again.

Here's a excerpt from . . .
Sweet Valley High #122
A Kiss Before Dying
Available now wherever books are sold.

Elizabeth Wakefield was trapped in a nightmare of flashing lights, polices sirens and angry shouting. All around her, guys with bruises and bloodstained faces were being handcuffed and pushed into police cars. Her own boyfriend, Todd Wilkins, had been arrested and was on his way to jail. Right next to her, a policeman's radio switched on, startling her with a sudden burst of crackling static.

Elizabeth wrapped her green sweater tighter around herself, overlapping its front edges, and then folded her arms over her chest, as if to protect herself from the chaos. Someone bumped her from behind. She turned to see a tall, scowling police officer pushing two handcuffed guys ahead of him, one whose neck was bleeding profusely.

A few yards away, Bruce Patman was lying facedown on the ground as a female officer stood over him, reading him his rights. Elizabeth had known

1

Bruce since childhood. He did have a hot temper and reckless side, but it shocked her to see him treated like a dangerous criminal.

Elizabeth had called the police because she suspected something terrible was going to happen tonight. And she had been right. It'd been every bit as terrible as she'd feared.

Enid Rollins, her best friend, stepped up beside her. "This is so awful," Enid said, a look of horror on her face. "How could an argument over a football game escalate into an all-out riot?"

"It's unbelievable, isn't it? I don't think Todd is ever going to forgive me for calling the police."

"I'm sure Todd didn't mean what he said to you, Liz."

"Didn't he?" Elizabeth whispered, overcome with a feeling of sadness. She had offered to go to the police station to help him, but Todd wanted nothing to do with her. His parting words as the police officers had pushed him into the back seat of the cruiser echoed in her mind: "Don't do me any favors!" Elizabeth exhaled a shaky breath, a dark heaviness squeezing her chest. "I don't know what to believe anymore."

"He'll calm down soon enough," Enid mumbled.

Elizabeth wasn't convinced, but she appreciated the reassuring gesture anyway. She knew Enid was trying to be supportive.

How could an argument over a football game turn into this? Elizabeth wondered. A few weeks ago, their school's football team, the Sweet Valley High Gladiators, had lost a game against the Palisades High

2

Pumas, who had played dirty. Since then, the guys of both schools had been locked in a vicious rivalry, with agression and retaliation bouncing back and forth between them like ping-pong balls.

Tonight, the guys from Palisades had tricked the SVH class clown, Winston Egbert, into driving out to an abondoned warehouse on the outskirts of Sweet Valley. The guys from SVH had learned of the deception and rushed to Winston's rescue—but not before Winston had been seriously beaten.

Elizabeth, Enid and a few other girls from Sweet Valley had arrived at the warehouse a short time later to find a battle raging like a scene from a cheap adventure movie—guys punching, shoving, brandishing sticks, staggering, blood dripping from their noses and cracked lips. Elizabeth shuddered, remembering. She would never have imagined Todd being capable of violence. But tonight she had seen a side of him that terrified her—a dark, vicious animal had replaced the sweet, gentle guy she loved.

"I'm going to go look for Maria and Winston," Enid said, breaking into Eliabeth's thoughts. "Will you be all right?"

Elizabeth nodded. "Go ahead. I'll catch up with you guys in a minute. I want to look for Jessica. I thought I saw her standing in the shadows on the other side of the building a little while ago."

Enid walked away without making a disparaging comment at the mention of Jessica's name, for which Elizabeth was grateful. It wasn't any secret that Enid and Jessica didn't like each other. Enid considered

Jessica to be shallow and self-centered, and in some ways the labels fit. Jessica and Elizabeth were identical twins, but only in appearance. Their personalities were miles apart. Unlike her sister, Elizabeth was a conscientious student and set high goals for herself. Although she and Jessica were only in their junior year of high school, Elizabeth already knew that she wanted to be a professional writer someday. She was actively involved in her school's newspaper, *The Oracle*, as a reporter and as the writer of a weekly column. During her free time, Elizabeth enjoyed reading poetry, watching old movies, hanging out with Enid, or going on quiet, romantic dates with Todd.

Jessica lived for the moment. The most important goal in her life was having fun, which for her meant shopping, dressing up, partying, flirting, and competing for attention. And Jessica thought Enid was the most pathetic nerd she'd ever met and couldn't understand why Elizabeth allowed herself to be seen with such a loser.

Even under normal conditions, Elizabeth found Enid and Jessica's attitude toward each other to be somewhat irritating. But tonight, with so much free-floating hostility already in the air, Elizabeth couldn't bear to deal with personality conflicts as well.

While Jessica took life to be one great adventure, Elizabeth hung back, giving serious consideration to her actions. Although she had been born only four minutes before Jessica, Elizabeth was clearly the older sister. The job seemed to require a certain amount of worrying about Jessica, who rarely gave a thought to caution or common sense. Elizabeth had saved Jessica from more tight spots than she could count.

Jessica had been acting mysterious lately and Elizabeth knew that was a bad sign. Something was up with her younger sister and that could only mean trouble.

Lila Fowler and Amy Sutton, two of Jessica's best friends, were sitting on the hood of Lila's green Triumph, which was parked across the street. Elizabeth crossed the narrow gravel road and walked over to them.

Lila, Amy, Elizath, Enid, and Maria Santelli had rushed to the scene that evening in a desperate attempt to stop the violence. They'd all been at the Dairi Burger, a popular hang-out in Sweet Valley, when they'd heard the news that Winston had been trapped by the Palisades guys.

Lila and Amy had spread a Persian rug over the car, probably so that Lila wouldn't soil her designer silk skirt. They appeared to be watching the goings-on with detached interest, as if they had the best seats at a sporting event.

"Have you seen Jessica?" Elizabeth asked.

"Yes, she was standing right there," Lila said. Her gold bracelet sparkled as she pointed to a grassy spot a few yards up the street. "We called her, but she ignored us," she added, her voice bitter. "Jessica has been acting so weird lately. I'm getting sick of it."

Amy's slate-gray eyes flashed with anger. "So am I," she said. "Who does Jessica think she is, anyway?"

5

"Where did she go?" Elizabeth asked, ignoring their commentary.

"She took off in a blue Volkswagen bus," Amy said. "I have no idea who she was with. I couldn't see the driver and I didn't recognize the vehicle."

Elizabeth felt a gnawing urgency growing inside her. "About how long ago was it?"

Lila and Amy looked at each and shrugged. "I don't know," Lila answered, "twenty minutes, maybe."

"That's about right," Amy agreed. "But I still can't believe she just took off without saying one word to us. Wait till I see her. This mystery act of hers is starting to get on my nerves."

"If she comes back, tell her I'm looking for her," Elizabeth said, wishing desperately that she knew where Jessica was. The hopeful thought that she might already be safe at home occured to Elizabeth. But years of experience warned her that it was more likely Jessica had gotten herself into another one of her infamous jams.

"Okay, but how long do we have to stay here?" Amy said impatiently. "The action seems to be dying down and I'd like to leave soon."

Amy's callous remark annoyed Elizabeth, and Lila too, it seemed. She glared at Amy, then turned to Elizabeth. "The thrill is gone, I guess," Lila said sarcastically.

Gazing at the scene across the street, Elizabeth reluctantly admitted to herself that there didn't seem to be much reason to stay. Most of the cars had cleared out of the lot and only two police cruisers remained.

"I guess there's nothing left to do here," Elizabeth said. Jessica was probably long gone and wouldn't be coming back. "I'll go find Enid and Maria."

Jessica Wakefield sighed contentedly as she watched the shadows move across Christian Gorman's face as he drove. He steered the van with one hand, the other one loosely entwined with hers in the space between the bucket seats.

They'd left the scene at the abandoned warehouse nearly an hour ago. After a long, aimless drive along the California coast, they were headed back to Sweet Valley. Neither one had spoken much, but words weren't necessary between them. The touch of Christian's hand and the look in his eyes when he glanced sideways at her communicated louder than words ever could. A feeling of love swelled in her heart. She was struck with the awesome awareness of being more alive than she'd ever felt in her life.

She only wished the dark, warm cocoon of Christian's van could shelter them forever. "I never want to go back to Sweet Valley," she said, breaking the silence.

Christian's lip twitched with the hint of a smile, but he said nothing.

"I mean it," she said.

He responded with a gentle squeeze of her hand. She smiled softly and turned to gaze at the passing scenery. The ocean shimmered in the moonlight, its vastness tugging at her heart. It was the ocean that had brought her and Christian together.

Jessica had been trying to teach herself to surf for an upcoming competition that she was determined to win. Her first attempt had turned out to be a disaster. She had wiped out badly and lost her surfboard in the process. After she'd nearly drowned, she had washed up on the shore, sputtering and coughing.

A shadow had fallen over her as she lay there feeling sorry for herself. When she'd looked up, she had seen the most incredible, gorgeous hunk standing over her with his arm around her surfboard.

Was it really only a few weeks ago? she wondered in amazement. She turned and studied Christian's movements as he downshifted for a turn. The muscles in his arm were rock-hard, she knew, and his skin was smooth and golden. It hardly seemed possible that she'd known him for such a short time.

He had offered to teach her to surf and Jessica had marveled at her luck. As they began meeting at the beach in the early hours of the morning to practice, their feelings for each other quickly deepened, blossoming into something more than either of them had expected. Jessica had never experienced anything so wonderful in her entire life.

There was just one problem. Their timing stunk.

Jessica already had a boyfriend. She'd been dating Ken Matthews, Sweet Valley High Gladiators' football captain for some time. She and Christian had decided not to talk about what they did and who they were away from the beach. By telling each other only a few sketchy details of their lives, it had seemed as though their relationship existed apart from their everyday world. That was how Jessica had fooled herself into believing that seeing Christian behind Ken's back wasn't quite so bad, that she hadn't been exactly cheating on her boyfriend. Christian had been a fantasy, a sort of 'mini-vacation' from reality.

Trouble was, reality had crashed into the fantasy, like an angry tidal wave smashing against a sand castle. A feud had broken out after a football game between the Sweet Valley High Gladiators and a rival team from a nearby town, the Palisades Pumas. Jessica and the other SVH cheerleaders had been horrified at the dirty tricks the Pumas used to beat the Gladiators. Several key members of the Sweet Valley High team had suffered injuries and in the final seconds of the game, the Puma's quaterback had kneed Ken in the stomach, knocking the wind out of him as he was about to make what would have been a winning pass.

As Ken became more involved in the battle betwen SVH and Palisades, Jessica spent more time surfing with Christian. But their individual worlds, which they'd tried to keep apart, soon collided. In a cruel stroke of irony, Christian Gorman turned out to be the leader of the Palisades High gang.

Jessica closed her eyes and groaned. Only a few hours ago, she'd been flying high with excitement in anticipation of her and Christian's first nighttime date. She'd carefully selected her outfit—a sheer and utterly sexy, gauzy green dress. She'd dabbed on her favorite perfume, *Rendezvous*, which she'd borrowed from Elizabeth. It was supposed to have been the most romantic Saturday night date of all time.

But everything had fallen apart so fast, it made her head spin. Ken had followed them to the Beachcomber Cafe, a seaside restaurant where she and Christian had planned to have an intimate, romantic candlelight dinner. Christian had been worried that something bad was going to happen that night, but Jessica had brushed aside his concerns and assured him that when they reached the restaurant, she'd give him a kiss that would drive everything else out of his mind.

She had been delivering on her promise in the foyer of the restaurant when Ken arrived. One minute, she was lost in the delicious sensations of a deep kiss—the next minute, she was looking up at Ken, his face pale with shock.

Jessica closed her eyes again, squeezing them shut. The image of Ken's stricken face tortured her. Their relationship was over, she knew that, but she cursed herself for not being up front with him from the start. Ken had been her friend before they started going together. He deserved better from her. What a mess she'd created!

"You don't think I'm serious, but I am," she said, glancing at Christian. "I really don't want to go back. Ever."

"We have to," Christian said, keeping his gaze focused on the road.

"No, we don't. Let's keep driving down the coast until we get to Mexico," she said, her words tumbling

10

out with excitement as her mind painted a marvelous fantasy. "We'll find ourselves a secluded beach where no one will bother us. It would be so romantic, Christian. We could live in the van, surf every day, feast on tropical fruit and fresh fish . . ."

"I like fish," Christian said, playing along. "But no eels; I refuse to eat eels. And I'm allergic to shellfish."

"That's perfectly okay," she said. "You get to decide what we have for dinner."

"Really?"

"Yes, of course," she said.

He looked surprised. "That's very nice of you," he said.

"Seems only fair," she said, turning to him with a look of mock innocence. "You're the one who'll be doing all the cooking. It's my fantasy, remember."

He chuckled, a low sweet sound that she found irresistibly sexy. "You're something else, Jessica."

"Thanks, I think." She sighed wistfully, tears gathering in her eyes. "It would be heaven if we could always be together."

Christian brought her hand to his lips and kissed her. "I wish we could," he said. "Being with you, Jessica—" He paused, taking in a deep, shaky breath. "We have to do things right," he said. "I don't want to mess up the best thing that's ever happened to me."

"I feel the same way," Jessica said. She knew the time for fantasies and games was over now. They had to return to reality and face it head-on, whether they wanted to or not.

"Come on, pal, get in there." A white-haired police officer with thick arms and enormous hands shoved Todd Wilkins into a jail cell and slammed the door shut. The metallic clanging sound echoed through Todd's head, which already hurt more than he'd thought possible.

A sharp stab of panic shot through him as he realized what was happening. He was being locked up, caged like a wild beast. The dingy gray walls and dim light seem to reflect and magnify his feeling of hopelessness. He wanted to scream, or weep—anything to stop the raging storm in his brain.

The policeman was standing on the other side of the bars, his legs spread out, his thick fists pressed against his lumpy hips. He was glaring at Todd with eyes as brown and cold as dirt. Todd suspected he had a mean streak larger than the gut that hung over his gun belt. "Now let's see if you smart boys know what's good for you," the policeman growled. "If there's any fighting—or anything that even looks, sounds or smells like fighting, I'll get mad. And trust me boys, you don't want to make me mad."

Todd watched him walk away, wondering what he'd meant. Then he heard a sound behind him and turned around, discovering he wasn't the only one in the cell. Three other guys were in there with him. Bruce Patman was sitting on the floor in a shadowy corner, his back against the wall. Two guys from Palisades were sitting on a wooden bench on the other side of the cell. They were staring at him, whispering to each other and laughing.

Either they weren't as upset as he was or they were better at hiding it, Todd figured. He went over to Bruce and crouched down beside him.

"How're you doing, man?" Bruce whispered.

Todd shrugged, scooting over to rest his back against the wall next to Bruce. "I've been better," Todd said. He pulled his knees up and rubbed his ankle. He'd suffered an ankle injury during a basketball game and had only been out of the cast a few weeks. Once again, it struck him how ill-suited he was for all this gang warfare.

"Yeah, I've been better, too," Bruce said, his gaze locked on the guys across the cell.

Todd recognized one of them as Greg McMullen, the Pumas' quarterback. Greg was the main instigator of the trouble, in Todd's opinion. It wasn't enough that he'd kneed Ken Matthews in the stomach during the Gladiators-Pumas football game, knocking the wind out of him; after the game, Greg and his friends had come after Ken again in the parking lot, taunting him with the name 'little windbag.' Then Greg had attacked him again, punching Ken in the stomach without provocation. Since then, one thing had led to another, and now here they were.

Todd wanted to believe that Sweet Valley High was right and Palisades was wrong, but what difference did it make? They'd all ended up in the same place, locked in the same jail cell. He was ready to put an end to the fighting. Maybe if he and Bruce could talk things out with Greg and the other guy, they could work out a compromise.

13

Bruce had shut his eyes and he was snoring softly. Todd nudged him with an elbow to the ribs. "Wake up, Patman," he whispered urgently.

Bruce opened one eye and turned to him. "This better be good. I was having an incredible dream."

"I've been thinking," Todd began. "Maybe it's time we stop—"

"So where's your dorky friend, guys?" Greg Mc-Mullen taunted, interrupting Todd's sentence. "Where's the little windbag, Ken Matthews? Guess he was too wimpy to show up tonight, huh?"

"Maybe he has a tummy ache," the other one said in a whiny voice. "He gets them often, doesn't he?"

"Can you believe he's the captain of the team?" Greg asked. "No wonder the Gladiators are such losers."

"Yeah!" his friend said. "Good old windbag. The cheerleaders yell, 'Go team go,' and this Ken Matthews—" He grabbed his stomach and began making loud wheezing noises, poking fun at the way Ken had struggled for air after Greg's attack during the game. The two PH guys laughed hysterically and slapped hands, congratulating themselves.

Todd glared at them, the blood in his veins boiling hot. Who do they think they are, talking about Ken that way? They were nothing but slugs who made the world a scummy place. Todd's hope for peace was replaced with a blinding rage. His control snapped. He leaped toward the PH guys, barely conscious of his movements. The wooden bench toppled over with a crash. Todd pinned Greg's arms to the floor with his

14

legs and smashed his fist into the jerk's face again and again, aware of nothing but the thudding sound of flesh hitting flesh and the scraping sensation against his knuckles.

Suddenly two strong arms gripped Todd from behind and dragged him off of Greg. Todd struggled to get free, shoving and pushing his body against his captor.

"Take it easy, smart boy," a familiar voice growled in his ear. The next thing he heard was the click of handcuffs. A strong hand grabbed his shoulder and shoved him toward the door of the cell. "We'll teach you how to play rough if that's what you want, kid." Todd turned and looked into the hard, gloating eyes of the white-haired policeman.

"I told you not to make me mad," the man said, a cruel grin splitting his face.

Once again, Todd was painfully aware of everything around him. He's hands were locked behind his back and a police officer was dragging him away by the collar. *I'm not a criminal!* his mind screamed. *I'm a nice kid, really. I don't belong in jail.*

The policeman opened the door of a small cell and pushed Todd inside, hard enough to knock him to the floor. "Let me know if you start itching for another fight, smart boy," he said as he leaned over Todd and removed the handcuffs. Then he locked the cell and walked away, the sound of his jeering laughter ringing through the narrow corridor.